You Don't Have to

FORWARD
TIME
EXPIRED

GODFREY WILSON III

outskirtspress
DENVER, COLORADO

Forward Time Expired
You Don't Have to be Crazy to Work Here... They'll Train You
All Rights Reserved.
Copyright © 2014 Godfrey Wilson III
v3.0

Outskirts Press, Inc.
http://www.outskirtspress.com

ISBN: 978-1-4787-3777-3

Outskirts Press and the "OP" logo are trademarks belonging to Outskirts Press, Inc.

PRINTED IN THE UNITED STATES OF AMERICA

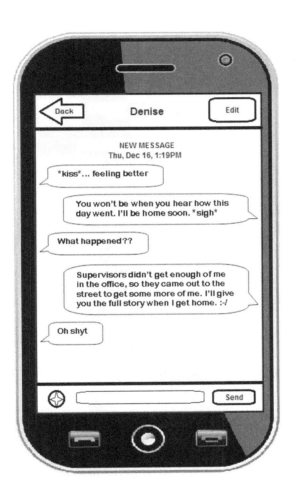

12/16/10 –
The Beginning

"No man is sane who does not know how to be insane on the proper occasions."— Henry Ward Beecher

"Tell me when you want me to let go of your throat…"

Before I could catch myself, every second of the past eleven years of mistreatment, harassment, and disrespect had all come to a head in the form of a lunging motion with both of my arms outstretched and a neck perfectly centered within the crosshairs. I already had her neck within my clutches and had backed her into a support beam in the middle of the floor before most of my co-workers even realized what was going on.

"I SAID, tell me when you want me to let go of your THROAT, BITCH!"

Knowing full well that she had no way of honoring my request, I increased the pressure. She began to flail around aimlessly, as her tongue protruded from her mouth, in search of any gasp of air in the vicinity to be had. A couple of men rushed over to intervene. A couple of women began frantically screaming for mercy. I had none. Even the reserve tank was on 'E'. And the men quickly realized that a man both possessed and determined was a bit more powerful than they had estimated.

As everyone who chose to get involved worked fiercely to break my death grip and as I enjoyed the rainbow of colors that her face was turning…she grabbed my forearms in a last-ditch survival tactic, dug her fingernails into my skin, and ripped away. I looked down and saw blood bubbling to the surface.

"Oh, that was the wrong answer, bitch…"

I pulled her away from the support beam and used her throat to fling her with all of the force I could muster, into a nearby file cabinet. The force with which she hit it sounded like a clap of thunder, and caused the cabinet to bounce into the wall with such an impact that it fell on its side and landed right on top of the motionless heap that was my so-called "elder" and "superior".

As others got in between me and the carnage to ensure that there was no further damage, I asked through a sea of redness and short, stabbing breaths, "So…what was that again? I didn't hear you the first time."

"I said, get over to route 9 and get it up! Maybe if

you'd get out of the middle of the floor and stop talking about football long enough to pay attention to your job performance, I wouldn't have to repeat anything to you!"

Emma knew that as of late she had been searching long and hard for my very last nerve and while she had probably been actively searching for face-offs with men ever since she'd retired from the military, she knew she didn't really want a face-off with *me*...because I was just the right one for the job. Far above average height for a woman and not what anyone would call a middleweight – or even a light heavyweight – I'm sure that she thought she was capable of kicking a man's ass. I just wasn't that man. I was just itching for her to turn her head so I could catch her eyes, but she didn't even stand still for the demand aimed in my direction, in search of someone else to badger...in her typical cowardice fashion.

It didn't really matter. Management had gotten so ridiculous with their attitudes and demands as of late, that unless I was asked a specific question, I had exactly three words for them: 1) "yes", 2) "no", and 3) "okay." I glared at her for a second, and then chose the response behind door number three. *That's why you won't retire. This job is the only way you'll ever in life be able to tell a man to get it up, you cockeyed bat...*

Christmas was nine days away, and we were getting

slammed with all of the online gift deliveries. The rolling hampers that held the packages for each route were neatly and numerically ordered in the middle of the workroom floor, some of them piled so high that the clerks had neatly stacked the overspill on the floor in front of each tub. Sheesh. I walked past them on the way to move to route 9 on the clock.

We all were hoping for a positive change to take place sooner than later. All we ever heard in the news on the mainstream level was story after story about how the company was "broke", and how there had been such a dramatic decrease in business volume and revenue. You couldn't prove that by our backs, knees and shoulders. There was an ongoing battle on the top level between labor and management about how restructuring needed to take place, from layoffs to eliminating or reducing service, and worse...which added to the uneasiness that seemed to hover over the workroom floor at all times.

In our station, the workforce was getting thinner with each passing day. We had already had two retirements this year, and even more recently we had just seen a rash of suspensions. Two co-workers had recently been suspended for an altercation that ended with a punch being thrown. One was back. The other was still fighting for his job. About three weeks after that incident, someone else was suspended pending a case of using a company fleet card for personal use. The days were the longest, the daylight was the shortest, the workload was getting heavier, the tension was getting thicker, demands were becoming overbearing, and when it came to who would do what, everyone was getting on everyone else's nerves.

To make matters worse, we had several unassigned and vacated routes throughout the station. A hiring freeze was in place, so no one who retired, transferred, or was disabled due to injury or illness within the past two years had been replaced. We had plenty of substitutes, but contractual stipulations prevented them from working more than a certain number of hours per week unless the workforce dropped below a certain percentage on a given day, so on most days we were covering the office work for one, and sometimes two additional people. Most of the people in our office would do additional office work, and typically it would be on routes they were familiar with, or held down prior to the ones they were currently holding down.

But sometimes we got stuck working on routes that we didn't know all that well – or at all – causing us to take much longer to get the route together. And today, I had the winning lottery ticket. I had barely taken off my jacket when my banter about the playoff picture was rudely interrupted.

I had all of the office work for route 9, which had

recently been vacated by a co-worker in search for greener pastures. Apparently we were too shorthanded for me to split the office time with anyone else, and almost half of the workload was left for today, in the hopes of less volume coming through this morning. No dice. I looked across the workroom, and whatever little relief that might have come by way of case work was instantly eliminated by everything from yesterday at the bottom of the pile, with a 'To Be Delivered Thursday' tag on it. I walked back to the time clock, clocked over to route 9, and headed over.

When I saw what was waiting for me, I felt my second sting of the day. Just recently, someone in management that was trying to justify their job had deemed the vertical containers attached to each case for the purpose of holding the overflow — which freed up our work space — unnecessary. So now, the only place to put what was to be delivered for the day was either on the floor or the case ledge. I noticed what was on the floor after receiving my marching orders, but couldn't see the case ledge until I was headed straight for it. The workload was stacked almost halfway to the top of the case. It literally stopped me in my tracks. I think ahead, and now it was my turn to groan. I played basketball in an intramural league and had a game this evening. I hated leaving my team shorthanded because of work. I hustled to clear myself some work space, then I got the

route together and ready to go to the str
as I could. I checked my watch. (9:41)..
the time that I'd be headed out the door
and I hadn't even touched my own route yet.

I was contemplating skipping my morning break
until I thought about my wife Denise, at home recu-
perating from an acute sinus infection that was causing migraine headaches. So the least I owed her was
the courtesy of a phone call when she wasn't feeling
well…and I was becoming more and more at a loss
for why I had any loyalty whatsoever to the job. As
I pulled out my phone and headed to the back door
of the building for some privacy, I walked past a line
of window customers that were waiting somewhat
impatiently. *Note to self: Google 'Stockholm syndrome'
later…* I pulled up the home number and pressed
'Call'…

"Hello?"

"Hey Love. You feel any better?" I asked as I walked
over to the edge of the dock.

Her voice was still full of sleep. "Hey Love. Not
really, my head is still ringing. But I'm glad you called.
I wanted to say good morning and tell you have a good
day, since I didn't get to tell you when you left this
morning."

"Okay, that's allowed." I smiled. "Are you still in
bed? If not, you should eat…or at least make yourself

a smoothie. Your body needs something to help you fight what you're feeling."

She groaned. "Yeah, I know…I'll get something a little later."

"You know that tonight's an all-nighter for me, right? Well…at least it's supposed to be. I might not make my game tonight. This holiday workload is hell and we don't have enough hands on deck."

"Oh, I'm sorry to hear that Love. I know you're committed to your team. But don't worry about me. Whether you make your game or not, I'll survive."

"Just in case I don't make my game…do you need me to stop at the store after work and pick up anything on the way home?"

"Break time's over!" The voice snapped from behind me. I turned around to catch Emma's eyes once again, but only caught a glimpse of a swinging double door.

"I can't think of anything at the moment, but if I do, I'll send you a text message", Denise said, recapturing my attention.

"Okay, I've spoken my peace…got to get back to work before I catch a case. Feel better Love."

She laughed. "Okay Baby, have a good day."

So now I'm almost directly behind the 8-ball. I pressed 'End' on my phone, and with pep in my step, I head to the time clock and move over to home sweet home, route 4, and head for my case. After the last round of route eliminations and adjustments – which added to everyone else's load – there wasn't much available space in my case for personal belongings. I used to have a third of the top row to play with, where I kept sunglasses, earphones, a headlight for late delivery days (like this one was going to be), gloves, band-aids, aspirin, napkins, rubber bands, and other tools of the trade. All of that was now sitting in a tub on the floor, and most of the space it used to occupy had new residential addresses, with the exception of one small opening in the corner of the last row. I kept a small framed picture of Denise there. I glanced at it, and sent a little comfort to her through the atmosphere.

I refocused, and dove in. The work for my route was just as heavy as route 9. The good news was that I knew it and could get it together much faster. The bad news was that I had additional door-to-door ad magazines that were supposed to go out yesterday at the absolute latest. When you have a door-to-door, it can't help but to take additional time on the street. Time I already knew I didn't have, as I looked across the room at the hill of parcels waiting for me. And the time clock on the wall refused to slow its pace...

I didn't even contemplate trying to leave anything until tomorrow. To do so would require permission, and that would require speaking to Emma. Expecting management to do you justice was a fantasy. They had extreme difficulty hiding just what it was they cared about, and it certainly wasn't people. Just as I made up in my mind that I didn't feel like pleading my case, Emma heads back in my direction. She passed by my case with her morning drill sergeant routine, carrying a clipboard and a yardstick that she probably wished was a rifle with a bayonet attached to the end.

"Will...the computer's showing that you're thirty minutes under, and the overtime list is maxed out, so I gotta give you some street time too. You'll have an hour off of 10."

"Are you serious?"

"Hey, it's what we're showing."

This witch right here... "Okay."

I got my entire route up and in order. It was time to tackle the packages. My average number of parcels per day was eleven. I had forty-six. But "the computer" says I'm a half-hour short on work. *Computers rock!* I pushed my hamper over to my workspace, and began to put the parcels in order of delivery sequence, and separate the smaller ones from the larger ones that would have to be driven to the residence. Back comes Emma from the other direction...

"Will, you've been running long on your office time this week. I really need you to get out of here."

This time around I didn't feel like waiving the right

to defend my work ethic for the usual form answer, knowing that I'd feel stupid afterwards for even trying.

"Shouldn't a little extra office time be expected?" I asked. "Christmas is nine days away. Look at all of these packages. And didn't we just have a service talk the other morning about how it's imperative that we make sure we go through the packages to check for mistakes before we leave here?"

"You can still do it, just do it on street time."

Yep, feeling stupid... "Okay."

I glanced at my lunch pail, and laughed at myself. I had packed a feast fit for a king...deli-sliced turkey sandwiches on whole wheat, sliced tomatoes with black pepper, pickle spear, peaches, pineapples *and* grapefruit, yogurt, and my favorite fruit snacks for in between everything else. All the while, hoping for a day that would be light enough to at least try and enjoy a rare lunch break. Now I'd be lucky if I had time to scarf down one sandwich between park points...and I began to realize that my optimism didn't stretch to the end of eternity after all.

I walked over to the time clock and moved to street time. I went back and loaded everything into my hamper; I erected my leaning tower of packages, and checked my watch. 11:08. Damn! I headed over to 10, Hassan's route. His cubicle was adjacent to route

11's cubicle, which was Kim's route. Everyone else had beaten us to the door by a slight margin on this frantic morning, so other than Emma and Liz, the evening supervisor who had just come in not too long ago, we were the three amigos still in the station.

Sometimes I would think that Hassan missed his call as a comedian. He was the co-worker that could command an audience, and have you in stitches with his storytelling in the break room. Always had a joke, a riddle, or a funny thing that happened to him on the way to the station...but he also had an encouraging word, a handshake, a sincere concern for what you were going through, and a heart of gold. Someone sorely needed for balance around this place. He was nursing a bad foot after losing a battle with Charmin, an infamous Rottweiler in his residential area that had seemingly learned how to open a patio gate.

"What's up Sugarfoot? I hear I got a piece off of you today."

"What's up Fresh Prince? Yeah, you got the apartments..."

I interrupted him: "Charter House, Winchester Square and Old Dominion. Right?" I prided myself on knowing the area we serviced. After a 6-year run as a substitute, there wasn't a single crack or crevice of street territory that I hadn't touched, I still saw lots of it via overtime, and I had a pretty good memory somewhere inside my cranium. So when Emma told me I'd have "a hour off of 10", I was thinking of the three streets that Hassan usually gave up when I worked a part of his route.

"Yeah", he said, "......and South Winchester Square, and Bankside, and Newgate, and King's Bend, and..."

My expression jumped straight to 'Highly Confused'.

"I got the whole fucking complex?!"

"Yeah, and they're trying to call all of this an hour", he mumbled angrily.

Highland Park was a large apartment complex that made up almost all of the residential part of Hassan's route. I looked down at the floor where he had everything that I was to take with me separated and neatly ordered, and what I saw rivaled what I had in my hamper for all of my residential addresses. It would probably take more than double the time allotted to get it all done.

Kim stuck her head out of her case and chimed in with a softer-than-normal voice so the supervisors wouldn't hear her, "Yeah, I don't know *what's* wrong with them today. And then they want you done and off the street by 5:00. That won't be happening, and they won't be hearing from me today."

That threw me for a second. Even on the worst

days, I had never heard Kim make a comment of that nature. She had one of the most kind and bubbly personalities I had ever known. Always positive, always upbeat, and always smiling…and had a great smile to flash. It seemed as if no one could bring her spirit down…not even people who appeared to be trying fervently. I worked hard at taking cues from her, because attitude-wise, she was who I wanted to be. I often wondered just how she always managed to stay so positive in a place that at times seemed just one small step above an asylum. But apparently management had succeeded in agitating the nicest woman in the world on this day. That's just what the office environment did to people.

Now I'm dejected. Supervisors were in the habit of dumping on us like this all the time, but this took the cake *and* the ice cream. Nevertheless, I always tried my absolute hardest to not get into a confrontation with management about the decisions they made. I usually just took whatever they put on my shoulders and let it work itself out on the street. I didn't want to fight, and a fight was what they lived for. So I decided I had better stick to the script, because I knew that their Modus Operandi was to get everything to be delivered that day off of the workroom floor first, and to catch selective amnesia second. What's more, I already was a little off-kilter about the 'running long on office time' remark that should have gone without saying, based on the time of the year.

"Okay, well…I probably better not add anything else to this trip", I said. "It's already heavy enough and high enough as it is. I'll go load this up and then I'll be back in to get my piece off of you."

"Okay Will. Sorry."

"Hey, don't be", I said. "You don't call the shots. You do the same thing that I do…follow instructions."

"You got that right."

So I headed out of the double doors that lead to the vehicle parking lot. I got my entire route out to the truck, loaded it up, and went back into the office to get my piece of 10, mumbling to myself the whole way. I stacked the trays in order of delivery, loaded them into my hamper and headed back out the door. Just as I was using my hamper to push the double doors open, Liz, the evening supervisor who was on her way to the boss's office, saw me and called out to me.

"Will, what time are you going to be done?"

I turned around to catch her eyes.

"8:00. And I'm not exaggerating."

Liz instantly yells out to Emma, who's now sitting in the boss's office with the boss, "EMMA! WILL JUST SAID THAT HE WON'T BE BACK UNTIL 8:00!"

Well I'll be damned…apparently the person that assigned the work can explain why it will take that long better *than the person who'll actually have to do the work. Hellooo? Over here???**

Emma struts out of the office, looks over at me, and tilts her head. I stood there, unmovable for the second, anxiously anticipating just how she was about to try and justify this ridiculously overburdened day.

She yells while counting and sticking her fingers into the air like a preschooler learning her numbers, "WILL!! IT'S 11:15!! 2:15, 3:15, 4:15, 5:15! IT'S NOT GOING TO TAKE YOU THAT LONG!"

I met her at her tone level.

"EMMA! I HAVE ALL OF ROUTE 4 AND **ALL** OF HIGHLAND PARK! KEEP COUNTING! YOU STOPPED WAY TOO SOON!"

"ARE YOU GOING TO RAISE YOUR VOICE ANY HIGHER???" She shrieked with bugged-out eyes. They had this thing about you raising your voice, even when it's directly in the face of them raising theirs to you. And if that wasn't bad enough, what was infinitely worse was that I was actually standing up for myself. The nerve of me!

I brought my tone of voice right back down to the level in which I answered the first question. "I'm through with it. 8:00. Goodbye."

I put the pressure on the double doors that I should have put on it sixty seconds sooner, and headed back to my truck with the second load.

I got to my truck, opened the door, and began loading my "hour" into the little crammed space that I had saved for it...and then started setting some of the residential packages that would be the first ones to come out on top of it. Then I heard Emma's voice from across the parking lot...

"WILL! DON'T DELIVER THE MAGAZINES!"

I froze. *...What did she just say to me?*

I'd had it. They had finally found my tipping point. After a decade of this same stupid shell game, this was the last straw. I backed my head out of the truck, turned around, and began clapping.

"Okay! Don't deliver the magazines! Great! You just saved yourself 15 minutes by switching to Geico!" I turned back around, closed the rear door, climbed into the truck, and plopped my butt into the driver's seat.

...and this is precisely why you don't question what they do, or get into a back & forth with them. No one is this obtuse. No one does this constantly and consistently without realizing what they're doing. Nothing changes except which mouth it's coming from. They want to talk to you like you're THEIR 8-year old. Just go.

"WILL! WILL!!!"

It's a trap. Don't look at her, and don't say another word. Get away from this building as quickly as you can. You're playing right into her hands. You can't say something nice right now, and it only gets worse from here. Get to pedaling.

I shut the door unceremoniously, in the middle of some sentence Emma was putting into the atmosphere, and started up the engine. I was just about to fasten my seat belt when I felt my phone vibrate and heard my text message tone. Not wanting to miss a message from Denise, I took my phone off of my hip to check the message. I could hear Emma yelling and screaming, but the sound was muffled and I wasn't concerned with what she had to say anyway. I saw that it was actually from Hassan.

"Try to keep your cool. Don't let them rile you up that way."

His message held me for a brief moment, but as I could still hear the muffled tirade of the psychotic woman a few yards away from me on the parking lot, it didn't last.

I appreciate you brother, but it's a little too late for that now...

I contemplated for a couple of seconds about whether or not to leave my phone on, because another one of their tactics was to keep dialing your number repeatedly, like a lunatic ex-girlfriend. I certainly was in no mood for that, but I didn't want to miss a call or text from Denise. *Ah, what the hell…I've already talked to her once this morning…I'll turn it on later to see if she tried to reach out to me.*

I shut my phone off, put it into my belt clip, shifted the truck into drive, and pulled out of my parking space. As I passed by the spot where Emma was hanging over the railing, I heard her yell my name as loudly and as fiercely as I've ever heard a woman yell.

"WILL!!!!!!!!!!!"

Whatever…

12/16/10 – The Middle

"*Anybody can become angry — that is easy. But to be angry with the right person and to the right degree and at the right time and for the right purpose, and in the right way...that is not within everybody's power and is not easy.*" — *Aristotle*

It was a beautiful, unseasonably warm day. Bright sunny sky, little to no wind, high temperature around 57 degrees. And I was getting paid to be out in it. For me, one of the perks of the job was the elements. We weren't so far south that we didn't get winter weather, but far enough to where most of the time, it wasn't harsh. Winter was cool. Working in it wasn't. So since we couldn't get ideal working conditions, ideal weather was a nice consolation prize. Liberty, solitude, the great outdoors, and the season to be jolly...days like this one made me tell customers "It's a good day to be working!" I didn't really feel like hustling hard to complete my work, but I felt like missing my game because of work even less. So I did what came naturally, and shifted into hustle mode.

I always made a concerted effort to try and shatter the average customer's perception of those in my craft: old, grumpy, inconsiderate, slow to help, disheveled. (That last one was a joke…I think.) I used to tell myself constantly, "No matter what kind of bullshit you have to endure in that office, don't you ever carry it with you and bring it out here to the customers. They didn't do anything to you, and your livelihood is contingent upon their loyalty…now more than ever." And on 95% of all work days, the standards I set for myself would melt away the insanity of the office and help my demeanor greatly. I wish I could have found it within me to let those same standards spill over to the brains of our outfit, but part of my efforts told me to meet people where they are. It was extremely easy to do that with customers in passing. With those setting the schedule that had shown their true colors time and time again, not so much.

The first hour of my route on the street was businesses. I was on the go, hoping to make up as much time as I possibly could to least have a prayer to make my game. I pulled up to the front door of my eighth business, put my vehicle in park, set the brake, reached over and grabbed everything for my stop, and opened the truck door. I was just about to hop out, when I noticed another company vehicle coming down a row at the far end of the parking lot. Then it turned at the front of the lot and started coming in my direction. Then, it pulled up to my bumper head-on, like the police swooping down on a known fugitive. It was Liz & Emma. They both got out of the vehicle, looking like a counterfeit Cagney & Lacey.

Okay, now it's official…I'm pissed. I was trying my absolute best not to get into a confrontation with them, so I made the choice to leave the confrontation at the station and just get the day started. Choice denied. Here I am, right back in the very position I was trying to get away from. I was going to learn my place today!

Emma walked up and positioned her body for the face-off that she had been dying for, and she thought she was the perfect size while catching me in a sitting position. She raised her right arm to rest it on the side-view mirror of my truck. Liz, who could have qualified for dwarf status if she was any shorter and medicine ball status if she was any rounder, put about six feet between herself and the truck and stood behind Emma, with one of her arms elbow deep into a bag of caramel corn that she just couldn't bear to leave behind, showing just where her truest concern at the moment lied.

"What the hell is this shit about?" I asked.

"What I was *trying* to tell you back at the station is that we were taking the extra street time off of you", Emma snapped.

"No, what you were *trying* to tell me is that it wasn't going to take me as long as I told you it would take to get all of this work done. Why would you have to *try* to tell me that you were taking the extra time off of me? No need to search for the right words if that was what you wanted to do...just say it. And *then* you told me not to deliver the magazines, all on the heels of *lying* about how much ti-"

"Don't call me a liar!"

"Why not?" I asked without missing a beat. "That's what you are, and that's what you do. Don't get all self-righteous on me now. Lying is the number one rule in the playbook, and you know it. Everyone knows it."

"We give that piece away to the subs for an hour all the time!"

"Oh, my GOD..." I rolled my eyes, and took in a deep breath. "You just don't know how to quit, do you? Look here...I've been doing this job for eleven fucking years, alright?"

Uh oh...the f-bomb...

"...You don't give that piece to *anyone* for an hour

because it's NOT AN HOUR, and you couldn't cover that much territory in an hour on the lightest work day of the year."

Emma scowled. "That's it...you're off the clock!"

"For what?!?"

"Because I don't like your attitude!"

"Ain't that some shit?! Well look here some more... you take people's kindness for weakness constantly and consistently, and then have the nerve to talk to them like they came to this planet in the last drop of rain. That doesn't tend to harvest bright, bubbly, sickingly-sweet attitudes."

"I don't need any more of your smart-alecky comments-"

"And I didn't need you to come out here and bring a bodyguard with you to keep this going. So here we are. Doesn't look like either one of us will be getting what we want out of this encounter, does it?" I asked with a smirk.

"I am giving you a DIRECT ORDER. You need to stop being insubordinate, RIGHT NOW. Go BACK to the station, and get OFF of the clock", Emma demanded.

Liz shifted her weight to the other leg, and inserted herself into the discussion. "Will, you need to do what you're told." I looked past Emma and looked at Liz the way a father would look at a child that just smarted off to him for the very first time. It must have felt like 50,000 volts of electricity, as her body jerked and the kernels of corn that were on their way to her mouth stopped on a dime. I knew without having to say a single word to her that from that moment, she knew to stay out of this.

I looked back at Emma, and grinned like a Cheshire cat. "I'm not going anywhere except into this building to provide my customers the service for which they are waiting patiently. Now would you be so kind as to please step out of my pathway so that I may continue on with my day?"

"NO."

I glanced past Emma and over Liz, and I could see Lynne – the receptionist for the company where all of this drama was unfolding – standing inside the glass front doors. She had left her desk and was trying to figure out what was going on.

"Well, then I need to see my union rep", I said as I locked eyes with Emma once again.

"You can see your union rep at the station", she quickly snapped.

"Not at the station, here", I insisted. "I need for someone else to see this scene *right here*, and how I'm being treated."

"Go BACK to the station, and clock out…NOW!" Emma shouted.

"I'm. Not. Going. Anywhere."

"Okay then…I'm calling the police!"

Welp, time to go… One of my guilty pleasures was police "reality" shows. I heard "police" and immediately flashed to a scene that consisted of me face-down on the ground, with a bloody lip and a knee on the back of my neck.

I positioned myself in the driver's seat and gripped the steering wheel. "Okay. You win. And I don't give a shit if you're happy about it or not. Get away from the truck."

I guess at that moment Emma could smell victory, because she took her arm off of the mirror and grabbed the door frame with her right hand.

"When you get back to the station-"

"Tell me about whatever I need to do back at the station when we're back at the station", I said while cutting her off. "Now back AWAY from the truck so I can close this door and do what you're telling me to do."

"Don't take ANYTHING out of the vehic-"

"GET OFF OF THE DAMN TRUCK!!"

Emma leaned forward and made strong eye contact with a devious look.

"You should have been fired a looong time ago."

I leaned forward so that my eye level matched hers, and gritted my teeth.

"If you don't get the fuck away from this truck, I'm going to mule kick you right in your teeth."

"Oh, well then let me make it my mission in life to see to it that you never again in life get back onto the clock once I get you off of it!"

Everything in my immediate vicinity turned red and hazy.

"Oh, well then let me make it my mission in life to make your efforts worthwhile..."

I slid out of the seat of the truck and acted as if I was going to walk around to the back of it.

Emma asked, "Now just what do you think you're doing?"

And like a champion black belt, I caught Emma with a side kick, dead on her chin. Her four front teeth flew in as many directions, and her body stiffened up like a two-by-four. I didn't even wait for it to hit the ground before I caught Liz's eyes, which had grown to the size of saucers. She would be much easier. There was nothing surrounding her but open space, and me laying Emma out flat appeared to turn her into a statue momentarily. I took a step towards her, and the bag flew out of her hand as she turned to try and run. The sheer sight of that was almost funny enough to break me out of my blind rage...but not quite. A part of me wanted to see if she'd set herself on fire from friction, but I couldn't take that chance...she might have gotten too far from me. So I trotted a few steps to catch up to her, and put all of my weight onto my back foot, so I'd have the right balance and momentum when I connected. She tried to scream, but couldn't manage to get anything to come out of her mouth. I wound up like a southpaw major league pitcher, and caught her with a perfect blow to her left temple.

I stood there, fists balled, with two unconscious women and caramel corn lying all over the front lawn of this business… trying to suppress the redness all around me. My heart and lungs felt like they were about to explode. I looked over at the double doors to the building. Lynne was gone from the door…I guessed to do what Emma wanted to do and now needed someone to do…get the police on the scene.

*. . . . . *Whoa*. . . . . *

All of the blood instantly left Emma's face. She let go of the door frame and slowly took three steps backwards – looking like she had just skipped up on a ghost. Then she stood perfectly still for about 10 seconds, and after the redness re-entered her cheeks… her facial expression changed from dictator to compliant, and she then chose the response behind door number three:

"Okay."

She headed back to the driver's side of the van, followed by Liz, who was reluctant to take her eyes off of me.

I shut the door, started the engine, buckled up, put the truck into drive, and pulled up right next to the van, so that my window was in line with theirs. I lowered my head to the level of their vehicle window, so that they could both see my face.

"And I hope you cave bitches choke to death on each other's spit tonight."

Way to keep it classy there, Champ...

As I was driving back to the station, looking over at the solid day-and-a-half's worth of work in need of good homes...I began wondering just what time some of my customers were going to receive some service... especially the businesses. *What happens in a situation like this? Why am I in this situation in the first place? All I wanted to do was get away from that damned building, see all of my familiar faces, provide my service to the best of my abilities, mind my business, and go home to my wife. Now people have to wait needlessly, because someone has to prove a point. This is stupid... Well, I guess I don't have to worry about missing the game anymore...*

Emma and Liz were trailing me. They had it... the threat of physical violence. Like the confession spilled by a captured suspect, in a heap of guilt, after a night of psychological torture inside an interrogation room...they had it. I posed a threat to a manager, and that manager had *another* manager as a witness who would corroborate her story. *Sir...your goose has been prepared to order. Extremely well done, to a blackened crisp on the outside...*

And it had to be by design. I couldn't have been gone a full fifteen minutes before two supervisors — not one, but two — had an epiphany that caused them to not only see things completely from my vantage point, but on this day, rush right out to get the extra load from me and ensure that I didn't even have to take it out of my vehicle and put it into theirs? I think not... the only thing missing from that fantasy was a sincere apology on bended knee.

They set me up.

I got back to the station and backed into route 4's parking space. Emma and Liz backed into a space on the other side of the lot. I opened the door to my truck, stepped out, and before I could take a step in any direction, I'm met at the truck by a woman wearing a badge. *Looks like the only thing that moves swiftly around here is discipline...* I do a quick survey with my eyes. Barbara, the boss, is standing in almost the exact same spot that Emma was standing in when I last heard her yelling at the top of her lungs, hunched over the railing. Chuck, the station mechanic, has his head poked out of the door that's kept locked, next to the double doors that we push our hampers in & out of. I wasn't sure if he was eavesdropping, using the door as a shield, or hiding a tranquilizer gun from my view.

I took a long look at who was in front of me. She was looking at me the way a customer on the street who was totally oblivious to all that was going on would look at me. She greeted me...

"How's your day going?"

Feeling like a flat tire, I replied with honesty.

"Shitty."

She smiled. "I know, I know, I know. I'm Susan." She extended a handshake, which I accepted, while trying to find a smile somewhere inside me.

"Hi Susan. I'm Will."

I looked down at the badge hanging from her neck, and almost simultaneously as I'm figuring out who she is, she tells me. "I'm a union representative for the office workers. Do you mind if we go over here to the other side of the lot and talk alone for just a minute?" She was one of the people sitting in the boss's office this morning when Liz called out to Emma, and just happened to be an innocent bystander to the beginning of this debacle. *She.....she's on YOUR side. Get it together, idiot...quickly...*

As we're walking to the other side of the nearly empty lot, Emma and Liz were walking in the opposite direction, towards the building. I shot the both of them a dirty look that they pretended not to see. Both of them were smoking a cigarette...I was guessing while in a post-climactic state of euphoria, like in the movies right after a steamy sex scene.

Susan & I get to the other side of the lot and face each other, with her back to all of the onlookers. "Okay, now can you tell me what happened out there?" She asked in a lower-than-normal voice. My shoulders drooped.

"They came for me. They gave me a ridiculous workload today and when I told them how long it would take for me to do all of it, they wanted to argue. I wasn't in the mood for an argument, so I just took what they assigned to me and left. Before I could even make a dent in any of it, here they come rolling up on me on the street."

"So you got into an argument while on the route?"

"Yes. My first mind was to leave that scene as well, to at least get to a place where someone with neutrality could see and hear what was going on, but they pinned me in and pretty much left me with no choice but to either make an extremely reckless vehicular maneuver to try and ditch them, or confront them then and there, on their terms."

"No kidding? So can you remember what you said?" Susan asked.

"Not exactly...I'm still a little frazzled." *You can remember exactly what you said. Good answer though...*

"Well you look perfectly fine to me!" she said with enthusiasm, in an attempt to raise my spirits. "So now that I can see that you're okay, will you do something for me?"

"Sure."

"I'd like for you to go over there and tell Barbara your version of what happened."

"No problem."

So we walked back to the other side of the parking lot together, so that I could face Barbara. With every step, my mind completed a lap around the Indy 500 track. Something within me wanted to believe that there was a deeper connection between the two of us that was somehow possible, seeing that we were the only two minorities anywhere in the vicinity. Unfortunately, she'd shown me time and time again that her allegiance lied with those who were perfectly fine with catering to all of her earthly whims...even if it was just a show on their part to try and stay within her good graces, because she was the boss. It wouldn't have mattered if they were plaid for as long as they kissed her ass just the way she liked it. Back during my subbing days, I remembered us crossing paths a couple of times at a distant station when we were in the same craft. At the time, she seemed more than nice enough, assertive, outgoing, and willing to help out with someone trying to find their way. I didn't know what had happened between then and now, but what I did know was that power and authority changed people for the worse far more than it did for the better...or maybe it just gave people the avenue to expose themselves for what they always were.

When we got to the sidewalk, Susan stopped short. I kept walking until I was almost directly underneath Barbara.

"Okay Will...are you alright?" she asked as she looked down at me with what appeared to be a concerned expression.

"I'm fine."

She worked her hands expressively as she spoke. "Okay, just so you know...I've already phoned the police." Then, before I had a chance to express the frustration that she knew I possessed behind her making that move, she immediately followed up with a hand gesture and an assuring tone, "They're not coming! Not coming...but they told me to steer clear of you if I thought that I would be in any sort of danger, and to immediately call back if I discovered I was. I told them, 'Will? Nah...I highly doubt that I'll be in any sort of danger, as I've never seen a side of him that even showed any anger.'"

"Okay, that's fair. I guess you didn't really know what to expect from me when you had only heard from them." I figured that Emma or Liz had already called her on the way back to the station, trying to do damage control and play the victims.

"Okay, good. So......" She closed her eyes and paused. "......what happened?"

I started from the beginning, and went through the entire chain of dominoes that had tumbled down up to then. I explained, "I'm just tired of people thinking that they can talk to you like you don't know anything about anything."

"I understand. Well here's what I need for you to do...I need you to take the piece of route 10 out of the truck, put it in a hamper, and bring it back into the station. Leave everything else in there."

I complied. After I unloaded the "hour" and was about to get behind the hamper to push it into the building, Susan intercepted me.

"I got it."

"You sure?"

"Sure I'm sure!"

That made finding a smile a little easier.

12/16/10 – The End

"Speak when you are angry and you will make the best speech you will ever regret."— Ambrose Bierce

We all walked back into the station together, and headed for the boss's office. Despite how nice it was in terms of aroma and décor (compared to the rest of the station), I hated being in there. The only good feeling I ever had before, during and after going into that office was when I was being interviewed for the job. Everything after that was for some nonsense. But this time around, management would be all in, and I couldn't fold.

Barbara, Susan & I walked into the office together. Barbara sat down behind her desk, I sat down in a chair facing her, and Susan sat to the left of me.

Barbara made eye contact with me and spoke first… "An inspector is on his way to take an account of what happened on the street from you, Emma and Liz. And I called Holly and she's on her way back as well, so that you'll be represented properly. So while we're waiting, I need you to begin preparing a statement of what happened on the street."

"Okay."

"I'd also like to prepare a statement on Will's behalf." Susan said.

Barbara replied, "Sure, that's fine." Her body language seemed to indicate otherwise. Then her cell phone rang for the second time in ninety seconds, and she excused herself and stepped outside of the office to answer the call.

I made eye contact with Susan, and humbled myself. "Thank you."

"Sure, it's no problem." She said with a smile, as her quest to lift my spirits continued. She was exactly who I needed to see, exactly when I needed to see her. *Wow…somebody who actually gives a damn about what I think, and how I feel.Who knows what would've come out of my mouth if management was who I had to speak with first. Thank heaven for large favors…*

While Susan and I were both writing quietly, Barbara came back into the office, fresh from ending the phone call. "Sorry about that…that was the husband. PTA meeting or Grizzlies game…touch choice for him to make, huh?"

We all laughed. Barbara sat back down, neatly folded her hands on the desk, and redirected her focus to me. Before she could begin speaking, Susan grabbed her attention with her index finger.

"If I may…you know, I have to be honest here. It seems to me like this whole thing has been blown totally out of proportion. Will seems more than calm enough and capable enough to go back out to his route and finish the day." She then turned to me. "Would that be an acceptable solution for you, Will?"

I look directly at Barbara with confidence. "Hey, I'm fine. That's totally acceptable for me. I was perfectly fine when I left here, and I still am. All I wanted to do was get to work. I can go back to the street." *… and enjoy a beautiful day that I'm missing out on while sitting in here with this foolishness…*

Barbara says, "We'll see. But for now, the inspector is on his way. He may want to question you about your statement. We'll have to wait until after he completes his report to make that determination." Susan complied, made a small 'well, I tried' gesture, and went back to writing.

Barbara looked back at me, and I grabbed her attention as well. "Okay, I only have one more question. If I don't get back to work soon…who's going to have to do it? I was already going to be out well into the evening with the piece of 10 added on. At this pace I'll be out well into the evening with just my route. I have businesses that I'm sure are in need right now." It was an honest question, as I had my already overburdened co-workers and more-than-patient customers in mind. I always tried to be the one who helped pick up the slack. Causing slack was a foreign concept to me.

Barbara shook her head and sort of laughed. "I honestly don't know the answer to that question right at this moment."

And so went the way of my 'well, I tried' gesture. "Okay, I'm listening."

"Okay so…Emma believes that you were being a little ridiculous with your estimated time of completion."

I countered…"I was asked a direct question, and I gave a truthful answer. I had given myself until 11:30 to get to the first stop on my route and get going. Then I gave myself six hours to complete my route. Now it's 5:30. Then I gave myself two hours to do my additional work on route 10. I don't care what you, Emma, or anyone else says…that piece off of 10 is not an hour. It's really more than two hours, but with the weather being so nice, I figured I might have a snowball's chance of motoring through it and finishing it all in about two hours. So now, it's 7:30. Then after I added in the travel time from route 4 to route 10, the travel time from route 10 back to the station, and time to stop and use the bathroom – because there was no way that I wasn't going to have to use it in that much time on the street – yes, in theory, by the time I was finished with all that, it would be 8:00pm. And that was being extremely lenient to your favor when you take into consideration the heavy package load, the ad magazines, and the assumption that the day would run off seamlessly and flawlessly. It never does. You know that. If Emma is the one who was in charge of the floor this morning, then why would she act like my estimated time of completion was so incredibly outlandish? She knew what all I been given. She's the one who gave it to me. Hassan told me himself. I told Liz without missing a beat that I wasn't exaggerating. It's the truth. Why is everyone in this place so deathly afraid of the truth?"

"I understand", Barbara explained, "But even in the truth you can't be yelling at your superiors and acting unprofessionally in view of our customers and the public..."

"I only yelled at Emma. And that didn't come until after she wouldn't leave well enough alone."

"Emma told me that you were wild-eyed, irrational, and seriously had her fearing for her life."

"So what did she come out to me for? I wasn't any more wild-eyed and irrational on the street than I was when I walked out of those double doors over there", I said as I pointed in the direction of the doors.

"It doesn't make sense to purposely take yourself out to someone on the street who you feel is threatening your safety, or may threaten your safety, when she was perfectly safe where she was and I was perfectly fine where I was."

Barbara stopped looking directly at me and turned to her computer to begin typing.

I continued on. "Why not just send Liz out to get the piece of 10? Why not you? It's not like they were going to be able to do anything with the work at that very moment anyway. Why not wait until around the usual time in the afternoon that they start worrying about people running too long on the street?"

I noticed out of the corner of my eye that Susan had stopped writing and was listening attentively, but still had her head down and her pen in a writing position.

Barbara stopped typing, held her palms up, shrugged her shoulders, and tilted her head to the right...in search of some answers. She stammered a bit before turning to look at me.

"Well...Emma had a right to do what she did."

"But it's not an issue of what she had the right to do, it's an issue of what makes sense", I rebutted. Barbara began typing again. "And since when does it take two people to pick up an "hour" of work?"

Susan raised her head.

Barbara replied, "Well...Emma said that she was gonna need a witness..."

"Ooooooooooh..." I slowly turned my head and made eye contact with Susan over the top of my glasses, as she gave me her Watson look and affirmative nod.

We both look at Barbara, who was now flushed as she steadily increased her typing speed, realizing that she just said something she shouldn't have said.

I asked in a most inquisitive tone, "Barbara, answer me something...why would coming to take work from me require a witness?"

Nothing but the sound of fingernails tapping on a keyboard.

I sat back in my chair, rubbed my chin, and answered my own question: *It DOESN'T require a witness. But harassing and badgering an employee to the point where he says or does something that will cost him his job sure as hell does. Hmmmm......* I could feel that slow burn inside of me begin to rise to the surface, as my heart rate increased... *Don't ask her if she told Emma and Liz to do what they did. She may actually still be an ally...maybe...* I had to use serene thoughts of my wife to calm myself down, before my tongue became my executioner in the moment.

So around this time, the inspector arrives. He came

in, introduced himself, and then told us he needed our written statements, and that he was going to go talk to the supervisors first, then he'd be back in the office to talk to me. Susan and I handed our statements to him. As he was leaving out, Barbara followed him, appearing to be relieved. Right after they were out of the office, Susan told me in a very low voice, "Don't tell him anything."

I felt a little more air seep out of my tires behind all of this newfound infamy and attention, as I stared straight ahead. "Man...I had a good lunch waiting for me today. Turkey on whole wheat, sliced tomatoes, fruit, yogurt..."

Susan chuckled. "Just trying to do your job huh?"

I laughed and shook my head. "That's all." Then I looked over at her the way a little boy who got caught with his hand in the cookie jar would look at his mother.

"I'm sorry to inconvenience you like this."

Again she reassured me that I wasn't causing any sort of delay on arrangements. Seeing how spontaneous all this was, I found that hard to believe. Nevertheless, I was extremely grateful that she was there.

So the inspector came back into the office and sat down in Barbara's chair. He said while skimming over the papers he had in front of him, "Okay...I've read both of your statements and the supervisor's statements............would you uh, care to expound on the "mule kick", comment?"

Eh, boy... "No, not at this time."

"Okay, that's no problem. Well I've made a note of your demeanor and what I've observed as well. Are you okay?"

My confidence rises again... "I'm fine." *And if everyone can see that I'm fine, then why is all of this necessary? Or am I just in the middle of everyone's "Don't make him go berserk and run to the car to get his uzi and come back in here shooting up the place" programming...?*

"Okay, well here are your statements back. I'll be outside if anyone needs me before your steward gets here. I have to make a phone call."

"Got it", said Susan.

Well, I can clearly see what the focal point will be in all of this...my reaction and not their actions.

After the inspector ended his very brief interrogation, He got up and walked out of the building. I could see him through the window, pacing back & forth on the parking lot while on his call. I said out loud, "I wonder what he'd think of me if he'd met me at a party or a restaurant or a sporting event, as opposed to these circumstances." I looked over at Susan. "Is that weird?"

"Not really," She replied. "I can tell you've never dealt with anything like this before."

"Not even close." I laughed out loud.

"They're for the most part trained to be as objective and as impartial as possible."

"Let's hope that's the case," I said, as I was becoming annoyed with this waiting game.

"Well, I really hate that I can't stay until your craft rep gets here, but now, I really do have to go. I have an appointment with another client", Susan said. "I didn't expect for all of this to go on for this long."

"No problem at all Susan. The last thing in the world I want to do is keep you from someone who needs you. I hate that these were the circumstances behind us meeting, but I'm so glad that you were here."
...but I do wish you could stay...

"So am I", she replied. "Let me make a copy of my statement for you. I'll write my number on it so you can reach me if need be."

She wrote her phone number down below her signature at the bottom of her statement, and then used the copier on Barbara's desk to make a copy of the statement she was submitting. At that point, something inside of me wanted to tell her just what I was thinking, but my practical side knew that no matter what she was saying, my dilemma was burdening her workload and my welcome had worn out.

She turned around and handed me my copy of her statement. I sat there and stared at it for a few seconds, and as I looked down at the bottom right-hand corner of the paper, I saw where she had written down her number. *She's really serious about assisting me through this. Something you just don't see that often these days, let alone HERE. . . .I have to let this sink in. . .*

I looked up at Susan. She smiled one last time.

"It'll be okay."

I was sitting there looking like a Bassett Hound, about to be put to sleep.

"Thanks for everything."

"You're welcome. Bye now."

"Goodbye."

I watched this mysterious Godsend walk out of my line of sight, and sat there by myself, in a few minutes of awkward silence. For the first time since I saw Emma & Liz coming towards me, I was alone again, but in a completely different state of mind and set of circumstances. It was a few minutes that felt like half of forever. *How did THIS day get HERE?*

Right at that moment, I remembered that I had shut my phone off. I reached down to grab it, turned the power on, and watched it for about a minute as it rebooted. A couple of seconds after my home screen popped up, the phone began buzzing repeatedly. I had four missed calls but no voicemails, and two missed text messages. The calls were from the supervisors' desk. One of the text messages was from Hassan, wanting to know how the incident had turned out, and the other one was from Barbara, telling me to come back to the station, not too soon after I'd left.

Just as I finished checking everything, another text message came through. It was Denise, giving me an update on her condition...

The Fallout

"I see it all perfectly; there are two possible situations — one can either do this or that. My honest opinion and my friendly advice is this: do it or do not do it — you will regret both."— Soren Kierkegaard

I was sitting there staring out of the window, over-analyzing every job I've ever had in my life, when I saw a truck zipping up the street in one direction, then across the parking lot in the opposite direction. Finally...Holly, my union representative, had made it back to the station.

She parked her truck in the space right next to mine, and hopped out. I watched her as she walked down the sidewalk to the end of the ramp, then I saw her walk halfway up the ramp and stop to get a couple more puffs off of the cigarette dangling from her lips, as the wind managed to find some space in between the strands of her long, dark hair. As I loosened the grip on the papers in my hand so the sweat from my palms wouldn't soak through and cause them to rip, I figured this place was more than enough to drive a person to smoking, and drive a smoker to double their nicotine intake. The inspector must have been somewhere nearby, as I couldn't see him, but I could see Holly's mouth moving after turning her head towards the building. Holly flicked the still-lighted cigarette butt onto the ground below her, and entered the building. The inspector must have led the way for her, because they came back into the building together. I could see out of the office door that Holly had gone to her workspace to get her notepad. Barbara had been at the supervisor's desk chatting it up with Emma and Liz, and when she saw the two of them enter the building, she left the supervisor's desk to meet her there. Then the two of them headed for the office, with the inspector picking up their stride right before coming through the office door like a legal team.

"Hey, I hear we've got some kind of misunderstanding going on", Holly said to me as she entered the office, in an attempt to make light of the situation.

"To put it mildly", I stated flatly. Barbara went back to her chair, Holly took Susan's place in the chair next to me, and the inspector remained standing by the door. I had already lost what little level of comfort I had when Susan was there.

"So", Barbara said as he exhaled, clasped her hands together on the desk, and made eye contact with Holly, "Will was given a piece of route 10 on the street, in addition to his own route today, as a result of undertime. He felt as if the workload he had been given this morning was unfair, and the time to do it all was unsustainable. Emma told me that she went out onto the parking lot while Will was loading up the truck to take the piece of 10 back from him, and he refused to acknowledge her at that point. So Emma and Liz went out together to get the piece of 10 from Will after he left here, and from what I've been told…they had words, which ended with Will posing a threat of physical…"

Barbara caught me with her eyes. I was sitting there, just shaking my head to the left and right.

"…violence."

Holly looked over at me. I looked at her, kept shaking my head, and said to her with my eyes, "I'm sorry, but that's inaccurate."

Holly looked back over at Barbara. "Emma and Liz went out together to get the piece of 10 from Will?" she asked.

"Yes," Barbara answered.

"Why?"

Barbara paused for a second or two, as her eyes aimed for the ceiling, in search for the answer to that question.

"Emma told me that she'd feel a lot safer if someone went with her instead of going out alone."

My eyeballs sprang out of their sockets. Holly just stared at Barbara.

"Well I tried calling Will, to tell him to bring the piece back, but I couldn't reach him by phone", Barbara added.

"Well, as I'm sure you're aware...using your cell phone while on the street is prohibited. So surely you weren't encouraging one of your employees to violate company policy...right?" Holly asked as she began to work an angle in my favor. I sat back in my chair and folded my arms.

Barbara cleared her throat. "Well...I felt that this here was a special case. An emergency even...yes, a declared emergency. And of course anyone can use their cell phone in case of an emergency."

Holly dug in a little deeper. "What made this an emergency?"

I could see that after that question, Barbara was beginning to get frustrated. Even though it seemed to be going well for me at that point of interrogation, I was beginning to get very frustrated. But I thought it best that I didn't interject at that point. Even though this didn't seem to be going anywhere fast, I figured I had better keep my mouth shut, even in lieu of a rebuttal.

"You know", Barbara responded as she shook her

head and shrugged, "I don't want to answer that the wrong way, so...I'll just admit that I really don't know why it was such an emergency. You'll have to save that one for Emma."

"Okay, I think I've heard enough anyway", Holly said as she pushed herself up out of her chair. "I need to talk to Will. C'mon, buddy", she said to me.

I got up and walked out of the office with Holly as we headed to another corner of the near-hollowed building, leaving Barbara and the Inspector in the office. Emma and Liz were back to irrelevant business as usual, at their desks in the middle of the floor.

"Will, Will, Will..." Holly said in the midst of a heavy sigh.

"Hey, I didn't start it", I replied as I touched my chest with all of the fingers on my free hand. Holly looked up at me for a second, and then shook her head.

We made it back to her tiny union cubicle in the rear of the building. "Grab a seat." There was nowhere to sit except her desk chair, so I trotted over to a nearby stool, grabbed it with my free hand, trotted back to the cubicle, set it down right next to the wall and perched myself on it.

"Now you know that what Barbara just told you is a complete fabrication, right?" I asked Holly as I watched her pull her ink pen out of her shirt pocket and begin to quickly go over my written statement.

"I figured as much", she said without looking up.

"Emma didn't say a damn thing about wanting the piece of 10 back from me before I left here. She told me not to deliver the ad magazines."

"Well what she told you out on the parking lot before you left here will pretty much end up being a wash. That's your word against hers. What *you* need to concern yourself with is what you said that can be attested to", she said while shuffling through a few papers on her desk.

"Oh, okay…gotcha."

"Dude", she said as she turned and looked at me squarely, "…mule kick?" I had to cover my mouth as we snickered together.

"I honestly have no idea where that came from, and I haven't had time to think about where it came from since I said it."

"Where was Liz when you said that to Emma?"

"Standing on the sidewalk, a few feet away from the truck."

"Fuck", Holly said under her breath as she tossed her pen onto the desk in frustration and leaned back in her chair. She clasped her fingers together and put them behind her head, and swiveled in my direction.

"Okay, first things first…make no mistake. They went out to your route to start some shit with you."

"Of course they did!" I said with enough passion to have to catch myself from getting too loud.

"BUT…" Holly said, "…this is the very reason why you always have to keep your cool, even when you know they're stirring up shit. Because they knew what they were doing, and the both of them will attest to what the other is saying. Who will attest to what you said or did?"

"Understood", I said glumly as I dropped my head in defeat.

Holly turned back to the desk and reached for her pen. "Okay, we're up against the clock, starting right now. So let's go over what you said here again: you asked Emma if she wanted you to mule kick her, right?"

"No, I told her", I said as I stared off into space, envisioning myself in the unemployment line.

"No…you *asked* her….right?"

I looked down at Holly, as she looked at me with an expression that said "This is where you begin lying to save your ass."

I froze for a few seconds.

"Uh…um, yeah. Now that you mention it, and now that I think about it…yeah, I did say it in the form of a question. Yeah, I just…asked her a question! That's all I did…"

"And you weren't really all that upset…were you? You were just joking around with that comment, right? I mean, there's no way in the world that she could've interpreted your words and actions as really being *serious*…right?"

Eh, boy... this did not feel good at all. My gut instinct was telling me to tell Holly to not even go down that road. Let's just roll with the truth, and if I get the guillotine as a result, then so be it. But I fought my natural instincts, and continued to roll in the direction that she was pushing me.

"I mean...yeah, I can see how she *could have* taken what I said the wrong way, but, no...I wouldn't have... I WASN'T...I wasn't going to do that, or anything like that. How could I? I was sitting in the driver's seat of the truck! You can't possibly kick anyone from that position...forwards or backwards...right?"

"Right!" Holly exclaimed.

"Gonna be much longer back here?" The inspector asked as he poked his head past the corner, into my line of sight. I suspected that he had been eavesdropping on us the whole time.

"We'll be right in!" Holly rang out. The inspector nodded, and disappeared behind the wall. Holly pushed herself away from the desk and said to me, "Okay, let's just go in here and see what they wanna do for the time being."

I felt like some worn out carpet. "Okay, I'm good with that." We both got up and headed back to Barbara's office, and once inside, assumed the positions that we held previously.

"Okay", Barbara started up, "We've got statements

from both parties at this time, and now we have to wait for the inspector's report, which will take about…?" as she looked over to the inspector.

"Fourteen days", he said, as that was the proper response to finish her sentence.

"Any chance that we may be able to get that a little sooner?" she asked him.

"Fourteen days", he repeated with a smile. We all chuckled. "That's just typical protocol", He said. "We don't want to give anyone any false hope. There's a lot of backlog at my office."

"I'm sure", Barbara conceded. "Will, there is just one more thing I wanted to ask you before we wrap this up…"

"Shoot", I said.

"Oh, I can shoot you?" she asked jokingly.

I played along. "Sure. Put me out of my misery. Quick and painless…right here", I said as I pointed to my forehead between the eyes. Everyone laughed.

"No, of course not", she said with a smile. "Um… did you call Emma and Liz bitches as you were leaving your route?"

Huh? "Huh?" I asked with the most confused of looks.

"I was looking over their statements, and they both said that you made a really nasty, really lewd, almost homophobic comment right before you left to come back here."

Oh, THAT... "This is the first time I've heard that", I said with the utmost confidence.

"This is my first time hearing that as well", Holly immediately added.

The inspector look perplexed.

Hey, this lying thing ain't so tough after all, huh? But you better hope to God that it's worth it in the long run. Feeling any better? Think you can keep this up with them? With everyone else? I'm betting you can't...dumbass.

"Okay, that certainly didn't sound like something that they could make up, but anyway...I have both statements, and so does the inspector..."

"Do you have Susan's statement?" I interjected.

"Yes", Barbara answered.

"Who's Susan?" Holly asked.

"An office rep that just happened to be here at the time that Will got back to the station", Barbara said, while sounding like she had hoped I had forgotten about it.

I turned to look at Holly. "She wrote a statement on my behalf, signed it and left a contact number on the bottom." I slid it out from underneath my personal statement and handed it to her.

"Oh, okay. Great! You forgot to tell me this, buddy. Make me a copy of this, please."

"Sure", Barbara said as she sort of reluctantly took the statement from Holly. "Do you have a copy of this one?" She asked the inspector.

"Yes, I do", he said.

Barbara put the statement into the copy machine on her desk, and then continued. "So, Will...after everyone has all of their respective paperwork, we'll have to wait for the inspector's report to be approved and mailed back to us, and we'll send all of that to you in the mail, via certified letter."

"Okay."

"And...we're going to evaluate all the information that we have at this time, and get the area manager to sign off on all of the statements."

"Okaaay..."

"And...in the meantime, you'll be on emergency placement."

"What does emergency placement mean?" I asked.

"It means you're off the clock for two weeks", Holly answered for her.

I fell backwards in my chair. "Now why did I get the feeling that the word "placement" has no business in the phrase "emergency placement"?"

No one had an answer for that one.

"And..." Barbara said with a sigh, "...I'm gonna need your badge."

I looked down at my smiling face draped across the

right side of my chest. With a deep breath, I reached up and unclipped the badge from my shirt collar, and stretched out to set it on the desk.

"We'll be contacting you. Be on the lookout for the certified letter."

"Okay."

"Thanks Will", Barbara said as she lifted herself up out of her chair and extended her arm for a handshake. I really wanted to grab her hand with my right hand, grab her arm with my left hand, and flip her ass over the desk judo-style, all while telling her about herself, but with all of these people around me, I felt like I had already been cornered as it was. So I rose from my chair and found a handshake against my will.

I walked out of the office and over to the time clock with an unsolicited escort...the inspector. I looked over my shoulder to discover him shadowing me, as I originally thought he was just on his way out of the building. But no, he was trailing me...more protocol, I presumed.

End Shift: 1:49

I draped my lunch pail over my shoulder, grabbed my personal belongings, and headed for the back door. I looked over in the direction of the supervisor's desks. Neither Emma nor Liz looked up from their work. I must have looked more defeated than annoyed at that point, because the inspector hurried his pace to catch up and tried to make small talk with me.

"Don't sweat the two weeks. That's just the mandatory time allotted for paperwork to go through all of its necessary channels."

"Can't help but sweat it so long as the leave isn't paid", I said. "Life goes on even when the money stops."

"Yeah, I hear ya", he said. "I don't think you'll have to worry about anything beyond the temporary hit. I read what they say happened and it sounds like there were enough mistakes made on both sides to go around."

"Really?" I asked as I pushed the back door open.

"Yeah, it's just a red tape issue", he said as he used his body to keep the door propped open while I walked out. I turned around and extended a handshake to him that I didn't have to search for, as I wasn't so disgruntled by the day's events to not be able to realize that this man was only doing his job.

"Thanks for all of your help", I said with a firm handshake.

"No problem", he said with a nod.

I turned and headed for the parking lot, with steps that weren't all that deliberate…a rarity for me. I heard the back door shut behind me. I got to my car and threw my essentials in the trunk. Then I took my lunch pail off of my shoulder, opened up the door, and sat it down on the passenger seat. Then, after plopping myself down in the driver's seat, I looked over at it with a chuckle. Turns out I was right: I *didn't* get to eat any of my lunch...but not for reasons I originally thought. I stuck the key into the ignition, but didn't start the engine right away. After the ignition bell stopped ringing, I sat motionless for a couple of minutes, in silence.

Did I just get fired...?

I started up the engine, and began my crawl home. While I was waiting at a red light, my phone rang. I unhooked it from my belt to check who it was...Hassan. *Aw hell, here we go...* I pressed 'Answer' on my phone.

"Yo..."

"What's up Fresh Prince? You didn't let 'em get to you, did you?"

"Yeah, unfortunately I did. I tried to let it go, but they followed me to the street."

"Damn, they got really bold on you today! So what happened?"

"I'm off the clock."

"Off the clock?! What'd you do, Will??"

I let out a heavy sigh.

"I, uh…I kinda told Emma I was going to mule kick her."

"Huh?"

I tried not to laugh, but it sounded funny even to me, so after letting out a little gasp, I composed myself enough to contain the laughter.

"I was trying to get out of the truck to deliver to a business. Emma was all in my space, trying to force me to go back to the station, so I told her if she didn't get away from me I was going to mule kick her."

There was a long pause.

"MULE kick her??"

Before I could explain any further, Hassan starts howling laughing. I wanted to laugh the same way, but the humor and the seriousness of the situation were having a tug-of-war within me. So I just sat on the other end of the conversation and listened to him laugh. After about twenty seconds, he caught his breath.

"Wait, wait, wait…I gotta call you back, man. I'm about to drive into a damn ditch messing around with you."

"Alright."

He was still laughing like a hyena when he hung up. I exhaled.

WHY did I tell this clown ANYTHING…?

The Confidence Game

"In Paris, when certain people see you ready to set
your foot in the stirrup, some pull your coat-tails,
others loosen the buckle of the strap that you may fall
and crack your skull; one wrenches off your horse's
shoes, another steals your whip, and the least treach-
erous of them all is the man whom you see coming
to fire his pistol at you point blank." — Honoré de
Balzac

I walked out of the building to discover a woman about
a hundred yards away, holding a sign in front of her. I was
much too far away from the sign to read what it said, or make
out just who this woman was. But I could make out that it
was a woman, and she was clearly holding the sign up for my
benefit, as she made certain that she was always facing me, no
matter which way I moved. So I began walking in her direction, to find out just what I needed to know.

Suddenly, a massive explosion — complete with broken glass shooting across the parking lot with the speed and force of an archery arrow shot from a crossbow — took place inside the building I had just walked out of. It didn't rattle me as much as I thought it would, though...I remained focused on the woman and mystery message for me.

Almost instantly, the sounds of sirens from emergency response units began to descend upon the building. The sky blackened. Hundreds of flashing lights were becoming more and more vivid. I was halfway to my destination, and I still couldn't quite make out the woman or the sign. The writing was very small for the cardboard it was written on.

Fire engines were zipping past me. Policemen began quickly stringing yellow tape around the crime scene perimeter, which the two of us were still within. News vans and reporters began setting up their camera sets on a nearby street. Crowds of people were forming and wondering just what had happened. Helicopters were circling the area. It seemed like the closer I got to the sign, the smaller the words got. I stretched my neck and squinted...it was Denise. My walk turned into a strong jog. She was proudly smiling for me. My strong jog turned into a full sprint. I finally reached her, stopped suddenly, and looked down to see what her sign said:

ONLY [7] SHOPPING DAYS LEFT UNTIL CHRISTMAS!

My eyes scanned the room...

I was awakened by Denise's voice. She was already up and in the kitchen fixing breakfast, while sharing a laugh from her phone conversation with a friend. Denise was your atypical career student...sat on the board of directors for the University of Memphis, where she also taught an evening class, and was in the process of completing her dissertation for her doctorate degree. She was also a former Army specialist, a better shot than me (which she loved to brag about), a concert pianist, and a hog rider. A few years my senior, but a natural beauty with great curves, and could put some women half her age to shame looks-wise. She was...a dynamic enigma. And I felt like the luckiest skunk in the world to have her in my corner. The both of us consciously chose to show up late to the relationship party, but still managed to find a rare commodity in the form of a gem. Fresh out of the newlywed stage of our marriage, oftentimes we resembled silly teenagers more so than mature middle-aged adults.

Somewhere in the middle of the night, nature just took over, because I remembered my eyes being wide open, staring at the ceiling through the darkness, well past midnight. But despite the dream I'd just had, it was already a good morning...I had bypassed the alarm clock and slept in. That was unheard of on a weekday.

Not having to get up to go to work felt a little

weird, and almost simultaneously, liberating. It was a long time coming, and I needed to know what it felt like to not be tied to a job, if only for a little while. It would have been better to gain that feeling under more positive circumstances, but maybe getting out from under the rigid structure tied to having a job — especially *my* job — was just what I needed to kick start some of the really good ideas in my head that would help me to become the ruler of my destiny. At the same time, I began worrying that my customers wouldn't receive all of their Christmas orders on time, and whose hands that task would be left in. Despite those in charge, and the office bullshit, I liked my job, I felt as if I was liked by those that I serviced, and I didn't ever like feeling as if I was putting any of my co-workers — or my customers — in a bind.

While I was laying there listening to Denise talk about last minute shopping plans and the aroma of bacon filled my nasal passages, suddenly the sounds of The Intruders' "I'll Always Love My Mama" began playing in my ear. I reached across my body, grabbed my cell phone from off of the nightstand, and pressed 'Answer'...

"Hey Ma."

"Hi Son. Did you forget about me?"

"I'm afraid so. What was I supposed to be remembering?"

She laughed at me. "You'd forget your head if it wasn't sewn on."

I laughed with her. Mom was always vibrant and full of joy. She was a hustler and a busybody, but mostly in good ways. A little burdensome at times, but only about small stuff, which I tried my absolute best not to sweat. She and my stepdad lived on the outskirts of town, about half an hour away. She was always giving me little tasks to do here and there, mostly computer or technology related. Her excuse was that she was too dumb to figure those types of things out on her own, but her reason was to spend some time with me. I didn't mind. Our time together was good, and our conversations flowed very easily ever since I was a teenager. She always gave me a nugget or two of wisdom every time we had a chit-chat.

"You're supposed to be doing my flyers for my bus trip", she said.

"Oh yeah, that's right. Do you have a markup with the latest information on it?"

"I sure do. It's been waiting for you since Monday. Can you come pick it up after work?"

"I'll do you one better. Can you do lunch today?"

"You don't have to go to work?"

"Nope, not today."

"They gave you the day off?"

Eh, boy... "Something like that. I'll explain it to you over lunch."

"You got fired?"

I couldn't contain my laughter, so it was her turn to laugh with me. Mom always managed to zero in on just what was going on with just the smallest morsels of information, and she could never take an answer at face value. She had to have the entire story, right there on the spot.

"Boy-"

"Ma..." I said as I cut her off, "...what time is good for you to do lunch?"

"Around 11 or 12", she said through her laughter. "I have to run some Avon orders down to the ladies at the community center."

"I'll take you", I said as I strained my neck to see what the clock on the headboard said.

[7:48] "I'll pick you up and take you down to the center. Then we'll go have lunch, and I'll drop you off when we're done. Sound good?"

"Sounds good! I can finally use my Red Lobster gift card that I got for Mother's Day."

Red Lobster was way out in Wolfchase, but I didn't care...that was Mom's favorite restaurant.

"You still haven't used that card? I had a sneaky suspicion that that's where you'd want to go. Fine with me, so long as you promise not to put a freezer bag in your purse and load it up with biscuits."

She laughed some more. "You know I don't do that."

"Of course you don't", I said. "I just came up with that out of the blue, on my own."

"I can be ready at nine-thirty." I could tell she was happy at the thought of us spending some unexpected time together, even though we were on the phone.

"Okay, I gotta make a run and take care of some business first, so if I'm not there right at nine-thirty, it'll be shortly after…definitely before ten."

"Okay Son, I'll see you then."

I pressed 'End' on my phone. And now came the difficult part…letting my loved ones know what I had done, what was happening, and the possible ramifications. Not really the ideal way to get some time away from the job, and not the ideal way to spend that time, but nevertheless, I figured I may as well make the absolute best of my newfound freedom. And since I knew that men are bottom line oriented but interested in the details, and women are detail oriented but interested in the bottom line, that is exactly how I chose to approach the situation when it came to the few family members that I would tell, or those who would find out anyway whether I told them or not.

I had kept my promise to Denise and gave her the full story when I got home yesterday and plopped myself down on my side of our king-size bed, without even taking my shoes off. She stood there and listened to the full story without interrupting, in stunned silence and with serious concern. And from there, her expression went to a smirk. And from there, her expression went to a desperate attempt to hold in laughter, with her cheeks packed to capacity with air, sounding like a slightly pierced balloon. And from there, her attempt failed miserably as she sat down on the bed, after uncontrollable laughter began escaping her. And from there, she went from sitting on the bed to sprawling out across my legs, with her arms outstretched. And from there, she went from sprawled out across my legs with her arms outstretched, to rolling off of the bed and hitting the floor with a thud. And from there, she hoisted herself up onto all fours, crawled around to the open space on bedroom floor, and, while making absolutely certain that she had my attention, did her best mule impression and her best impersonation of a mule kick. I rolled my eyes and looked at her with an expression that only a cartoon character could match. *So much for academia breeding maturity. Toss her into the same bucket with Hassan...*

I wasn't feeling so terrible that I failed to see the humor in the whole situation, but the burden of the possible consequences was much too heavy on my shoulders for me to get caught up in the humorous aspect of the story. Besides, I knew that I hadn't said what I said in jest, even if it sounded funny while telling the story. But since what was done was done, I did my best not to dwell on it.

I hopped out of bed, showered, got dressed, and galloped into the kitchen to not take for granted the kind of breakfast that I absolutely loved, but usually avoided to keep from feeling sluggish in the morning; bacon, cheese eggs, grits, hash browns, hotcakes with butter and syrup, and orange juice. A feast fit for a king whose only physical duty was to keep his throne warm.

I slid over to Denise and kissed her. "Good Morning Love."

"Good Morning, Baby. Are you hungry?"

"Like a wolf. Everything looks great!" I exclaimed as I opened the refrigerator and grabbed the ketchup.

She leaned against the counter and just watched me with this big grin on her face, as I positioned myself for the onslaught. "It's all for your appetite. I knew you'd have one. Do you realize you haven't eaten anything since this time yesterday?"

I stopped and looked at her. "Hmmm...I hadn't. And now that you mentioned it, I just remembered that I didn't even unpack my lunch pail. Everything that I fixed yesterday is still in it, sitting on top of the fridge. I better put that stuff in the fridge before it goes bad."

She smiled. "So whatcha got planned for the day?"

"Oh", I said as she snapped me out of my thought, "Going to go see Mom and Pop…let 'em know what happened. That way if the worst comes, they won't be blindsided."

"Aw, don't even start with the 'worst' talk", she said as she grabbed her coffee mug to come over to the table and sit down. "We're not even going to think like that. Okay?"

"If you say so. Now stop making me talk with my mouth full", I said after chewing my mouthful.

"Whatever. You'd be eating cereal if it weren't for me", she said as she set her mug down on the table.

"Too-fay", I said in an attempt to say "Touché", with a fresh mouthful.

"Are you still going to the Bowl Ball tonight?" she asked as she set her elbow on the table and held her head up with her hand.

I stopped shoveling food into my mouth again and looked straight ahead, but finished chewing before speaking this time. "Damn…I had forgotten about that." The Bowl Ball was a Christmas party that my high school's alumni association threw ever year, the night before the big Holiday Bowl, an annual game against our cross-town rivals. It was all in the name of raising money for scholarships, and, a really good time from what I had heard…because I had never been to one. I had to think for a moment, because while a party was good, and getting together with old classmates was even better…I didn't know if I felt like doing a bunch of truth dodging, which I wasn't very good at. But I definitely wasn't going to show up to a party blurting out *this* ugly truth.

"I don't know, baby", I contemplated, "I know I've been talking about it for a while now, but now that this has happened, I don't know if I feel up to it."

"I think you should go", she encouraged. "It'll get your mind off of mule kicking people." She turned her head to laugh at herself while picking her mug up to take another sip of her brew.

"Yes it will", I said as I wiped my mouth while giving her the side-eye, "But so will two weeks of unpaid leave. I'll see how I feel after I'm done with the day's events."

"Fair enough", she said. "Well, I have to get ready for work."

"I won't hold you up", I responded. "Breakfast is marvelous."

"Thank you."

"No, thank you. And you have a good day."

"You too Love."

So I kissed my wife goodbye for the day and finished devouring my feast, and then it was on to that business I told Mom I had to take care of. I jumped into my car, drove a few blocks, hopped on I-240 westbound, took that to the MLK Jr. Expressway, jumped off at the 'South Pkwy E' exit, made a couple of turns, and pulled up in front of the quaint little house on Ridgeway Street. I checked my watch. (8:42)

Pop was by and large, a fountain of youth. Born in the roaring 20's with a green thumb, a World War II veteran, still living in the house where we all grew up and still self-sufficient to this day. Still rose at 5am every day more than two decades after retiring from his local factory job. Not even a junior high school education, and he did the Jumble in the newspaper every morning with an ink pen. He grew all of his own vegetables out in the backyard. He got around better than a lot of men half his age. One of the smartest, sharpest and hardest working men I'd ever known…and showed no signs of slowing down. I was lucky to have him for a father. Pop would be the easiest to tell – if "easy" could be the right way to describe it – but also the toughest to deal with, after seeing his reaction.

I had a key to the house, and I used it to let myself in. Right after I shut the door behind me, I let out my traditional yell:

"HELLO!!"

And I got the traditional response:

"HEY!!"

I could tell from the trajectory of his voice that

Pop was in the kitchen. I hollered out, "How are you doing?!"

His voice softened a bit, as he could hear me getting closer to him. "Oh, I'm doing pretty good…just fixin' me a little grub. You hungry?"

"Nah, I just ate", I said as I walked through the kitchen doorway.

"So, they finally gave you a day off, huh?"

I had to get my feelings out into the open, without the humorous element. I laid the gloomy incident on him without beating around the bush for even one sentence.

"No, not exactly. I'm in some trouble. I got suspended for threatening a superior on the street."

He looked over at me, and his eyes instantly filled with pain the second that my words sunk in. He put his breakfast on hold and sat me down at the kitchen table. "What happened?" he asked sincerely. I gave him the essentials of the incident.

"Oh, she's that type of boss, huh?' He asked humorously.

"I honestly don't know what the heck she is", I stated with confusion.

"Well, some people in authority positions are the last ones in the world that should be in authority positions…"

"We get that quite a bit at the job", I said.

"...but then also", he continued, "...some people just have their favorites to pick on. She doesn't like you like that, does she?"

"GOD I hope not." He got a laugh out of the way I expressed myself with that one.

"Well don't feel too bad about it son", he said. "We all have our bad moments, and we all had those supervisors that rode our backs for a reason that was in their heads and theirs only, that they felt was good. I had this one supervisor back when I was at the plant who had a bone to pick with me, every single day... and I think it was because I showed him with my actions that I could never be fazed by anything he did. He would perch himself over the railing and watch me like a hawk, waiting to jump all over the slightest little violation. He loved to tell me that he wouldn't have to deal with any more of my bullshit when I was gone. And son...this was back during a time when standing up for yourself was taboo."

"Right, right", I acknowledged.

"But I knew I was a valuable employee and a good worker", he said, "and I also knew that my foreman was a good, fair, and honest man, and had my back. So I waited for just the right moment and I pointed at my supervisor's nose and told him to his face, right in front of the foreman, "You'll be gone before me." And he was. He was almost gone that very day, because I could see in his eyes that it took everything within him to keep from wrapping his hands around my neck..."

He told me about a couple more bouts that he had with his chain of command while he was in the military, and his own managers over the course of his lengthy career, and I made it a point to listen to him intently. The man was a walking, talking history lesson that could teach the world a thing or three about its perception of 'hard work', if he'd had a platform and the world simply chose to listen. Whenever we talked, I always learned something new. We always had good conversation, but our relationship was undoubtedly 'Man-to-Man'. It had always been that way, ever since I was a preteen.

In a way, I was actually growing to appreciate the suspension, because it slowed me down drastically in this microwave culture...took me back to a point in life where I had a day out of the week or a weekend day all to myself, before the workforce became so short-handed and thinned out. I'd use that day to go to the old neighborhood and chew the fat with Pop. My excuse was always to wash my car, but my reason was to spend some time with him. Still having him in my life after all these years was a blessing, and this job was robbing me of it. I stayed there for an hour. I never had that kind of time to just sit and talk with Pop anymore. And while I was in the moment, I really didn't care all that much about how having that much time to devote to our good old 'Man-to-Man' chats came about. I missed them, and I wanted that feeling back. I think he did, too.

I remember his final words to me on the subject: "Don't worry about it, Son; you're going to come out of this just fine."

After looking over all that I knew about his life, I had no choice but to believe him.

And then, it was on to Mom. I decided to take the scenic route, since I wasn't in a big hurry. I plugged my iPod into the auxiliary jack in my car, pushed play for Irresistible Bliss by Chris Botti, and let my smooth jazz playlist unwind. I reversed those two turns I made to get to Pop from the interstate to get back to South Parkway East, bypassed I-240 and made a left where Elvis Presley Blvd and S. Bellevue Blvd meet. Good ole Highway 51…the late night cure for all my ills back when I was younger. Long drives on a warm summer night with the moonroof open, no real destination, and some good music flowing from my speakers, always seemed to right all of the wrongs in the world for me. Left on Union, right on Danny Thomas…I knew the city like the back of my hand, and whether I was riding or walking, working or playing, the streets belonged to me. Left on Marsh, right on Harvester, left on Semple...

Mom was watching for me. By the time I pulled up in front of the house, she was already on her way down the driveway, with both arms full of bags. I held in my laughter as she loaded up the back seat with her Avon orders, and jumped in.

"Okay, now what done happened?"

And as soon as she asked me that, the laughter just escaped. She was leaning in on me like a teenager trying to be the first one in on the juiciest gossip going around the classroom halls. I rewound the story all the way back to when I was first told that I'd have an extra "hour" on the street while I was still at my case working, and I filled her in on every single detail that I could remember, pushing the 'pause' button on my story when she got out of the car to go into the community center to drop off her orders, and pushing 'play' when she got back in. We began our drive out to the suburbs, on a quest for a hearty seafood lunch. It was a nice drive, and I don't know if it was because I wasn't in a hurry, or because Mom had to stop me at just about every point of the story to get the details of the details, but we had made it all the way out to the Galleria and I still hadn't quite gotten to the part about being escorted out of the building. From the minute we got out of the car, she was joined to my hip. The story must have been really intriguing to her, because after we were seated in our booth, she was leaning so far over the table that there was nowhere for the hostess to set the menu down. As she excused herself, it was hard for me to keep my composure just from looking at her. She was so focused on me, the mere expression on her face was laughable, and she got her good gut laugh in at the same point that Hassan and Denise got theirs...when four-legged creatures came into the picture. I completed the details of the day's events sometime shortly after we placed our orders. I was so thorough with all of what took place that I actually found the story sort of amazing myself. It got me to thinking...I had a pretty good memory. And that would come in handy when I heard what I was in for later that day.

Meanwhile, Mom and I moved on to our usual topics of discussion; Pop, my stepdad, my sisters, church, and what was going on in the world, both locally and on the international stage. It was a nice break from all the trouble at hand. After each of us had soaked in all of what the other had to say, she sat back and relaxed a bit. She would always say it helped her food to digest. And then, she remembered what it was that we were originally talking about.

"So you really did get fired, huh?"

I rolled my eyes. "No mother, suspended. But I

have very little doubt that they'll be going for the kill while they have me on the outside looking in, because now I can't fight the battle. I have to depend on someone else to fight it for me. So by this time next week, you may be right."

I was expecting her to go into pity mode, but instead she maintained her stature, shrugged her shoulders, threw her palms up, and grinned at me. I looked at her with extreme curiosity and smiled.

"And just what is that supposed to mean?"

She smiled at me for a couple of seconds and said, "It means that it just might be time for you to let them have their red wagon back."

Whaaaaat??? I loved Mom's old southern belle expressions. But that most definitely was not what I was expecting her to say.

"Huh? You mean you're not worried?" I asked with a confused look.

"Not at all son", she said. "I've never worried about you, because you've never been the one to worry about. I know you. You're smart, you're self-sufficient, you have an education, you've found a wife that loves and supports you, and you've had a backup plan ever since you were in tenth grade. If it happens, then it happens. You'll figure out where you need to be."

"Wow..." I said as I sat straight up. "You really mean all of that?"

"Boy", she said, "You're talking like you didn't come from me. Like I didn't raise you…I know my children, son. Of course I mean all of that. But for now, you might be a little light in the pockets, so lunch is on me. Heh heh heh…" she said as she went into her mammoth purse to search for her wallet.

"Oh, you got jokes too?"

"A couple", she said while sifting through her wallet to pull out her gift card. "We've gotta get rolling though. I've gotta get these bus trip flyers out to my people. Thank you, by the way…"

"Don't you mean lunch is on me?" I asked sarcastically as I interrupted her thought.

"No son…" she said without looking up, "…lunch is on ME. This is MY card. I don't care if you bought it."

I laughed as I leaned over the table to peer into the purse while she was rambling.

"Is that a freezer bag?"

She cut her eyes at me. "Shut up."

***

After leaving Mom's place, I was still in the mood for the scenic route while driving home. I was headed south on Getwell Avenue, grooving to The Zodiac by Down To The Bone when a phone call interrupted the music. It was my co-worker, Chris, calling me. He was very active in the union, and I was hoping he had some pertinent information, but seeing that it had only been a little over 24 hours, I knew that was wishful thinking. I pressed 'Answer' on my phone…

"Hey Chris, what's up?"

"Man, I'm so upset right now I don't know what to do", he said in a huff.

"Well calm down before you do what I did."

"I tried, but that's kind of hard to do when I'm standing in that damn station listening to a bunch of lies. I've been stewing all day. Can you talk?"

I was waiting on a red light at Rhodes Avenue. "Sure, but I'm driving at the moment, so give me a minute to pull over so I don't create a whole 'nother set of problems while we're talking."

"Okay, that's cool. I just got back from off the street and I'm unloading, so take your time. Had to have some time taken off of me to keep it at eight, so I can get some grievance paperwork done on a few cases…and this is just one more to add to the pile. Man, we need you sitting at home right now like we need a hole in our heads. Already overworked and understaffed as it is, and they pull this shit. Ugh…" he said in an attempt to regain his composure.

As soon as the light turned green, I turned into the Walgreens' parking lot and pulled into a space facing the street.

"Okay, what's the scoop?"

"Well, I got as much of the story as I could gather from off of the floor - because you know everyone's talking about it - and Emma was campaigning all over the floor this morning talking about how you were acting like a raving lunatic, hurling boxes all over the street, and threatening to kill her."

"Hurling boxes?" I asked with a laugh. "Where the hell did she get that from?"

"I don't know, but that's what she said", he replied. "Anyone acting the way she said you were acting would have been half naked and missing patches of hair by the time you got back to the station. And I KNOW that you weren't out there acting like that. I just KNOW that not a single word of that is true...right?"

Eh, boy... "Well...you know how some people can really believe that their life is about to end because someone is yelling at them – and that has more to do with the preconceived notions in their head than the actual circumstances – but I have to admit...towards the end, it got pretty heated. And yes, I said a couple of things that I definitely shouldn't have said. But right up until the bitter end, Emma was all in my face, working hard at getting her digs in. So she didn't feel threatened...no matter what she's saying now."

"Well, sounds to me like she finally got her chance to piss on someone the way she always wanted to, and she took it", Chris said, engulfed in his own thoughts.

"You may be right", I said, "but what constantly baffles me is just how I came to be the one that anybody wants to piss on. When I first landed the job, I tried hard to find the good in everybody, no matter which side they were on. I didn't believe that there simply was no good at all to be found in certain individuals. I wish I still felt that way."

"Well they fuck with everybody, Will. Maybe you don't see it so much because as of late, you pretty much keep your head inside your work and stay to yourself all the time. Sometimes you gotta take a look around, if for no other reason than to understand that you aren't being singled out."

"I don't think I'm being singled out, but I do think that all of them make it a point to come at me even when I'm doing everything right. They bark at you about doing your work, but if you're quiet and working, here they come with nothing of importance, causing you to stop working. Does power do that to people?"

"It does, but Emma's problem is easy. You're everything that she could never be, and you're everything she could never have. The reason why everyone else is constantly moving from place to place but she's a mainstay, is because she's too stupid to pass an exam that would make her eligible for the next level of management. And she sure as hell is too old and broken down to go back to the street, so she's stuck with the flunky work and bitter about it. Were it not for our station saving her all these years, someone on the regional level probably would have forced her into retirement by now. Meanwhile, people know your background – even if you don't think they know about it – and people in the company that don't work in our building, who know the *real* you and not the hype that surrounds your name when any of these supervisors speak of you, mention you often when talk of who would make a good manager starts up. Emma's either a part of those circles, or word gets back to her one way or another. So of course, she has to walk in the place and see you every day, and I know that eats her ass up on the inside. And then, there's also the fact of who got you in the door."

"Andre? What's he got to do with it?" I asked.

"He's how you got the job", Chris explained. "And they never liked him. So they don't like you. Quiet is kept; they refer to you as 'Andre's boy'. That might be Barbara's particular malfunction as well, but she really hasn't been here long enough for me to say for certain."

And it was true...Andre was the one that got my foot in the door, all those years ago. He was yet another league member that we all knew, a little bit older and higher in seniority than the rest of us, but probably in the best physical shape of all. When he was in charge, he gave me an opportunity to break free of my self-imposed ball and chain desk job in the marketing field. He had since moved on to greener pastures.

"Andre's boy?" I asked cynically. "That's pretty stupid."

"They're pretty stupid…and immature. In some ways, it's like being trapped in high school for the rest of your life. Never mind that the people who matter – your customers – give you high marks. And you can definitely forget about letting your body of work speak for itself. Around here, it's 'kiss my ass and join the clique', or 'be your own man and get put on the shit list'."

"Well I'm definitely not an ass kisser."

"We noticed!" Chris exclaimed. We laughed together.

"Wow", I said "…I thought she was forever disgruntled about the treatment of women in the military or something. And come to find out that it's because of someone who's not even in the picture anymore? She doesn't like Andre, so she can't like me? Sheesh…I never thought that so-called adults could be so petty."

"Well they damn sure are. But anyway", he continued, "I got hold of Holly and she gave me your rundown from yesterday, so their hands aren't anywhere near clean with the actions they took. So you might have to cool your jets for a little while, but I have no doubt that you'll be back. And we're already getting unexpected help for your case from unexpected places."

"What kind of help?" I perked up a bit.

"Well, Craig — who told me to tell you that this is some bullshit, by the way — did your route today, and someone at one of the businesses gave him a letter to give to Barbara. Of course he was smart enough to make a copy to give to us first. I'm guessing this is the business you were about to deliver to when it all went down..."

December 17, 2010

To Whom It May Concern:

My name is Lynne, and I work for one of the businesses on Will's route. Yesterday, some sort of confrontation took place out in front of our building, when two women pulled up in front of his truck and they began having some sort of argument. He never made it inside, and we didn't see someone else until almost the close of the business day, who didn't really know any more about what was happening than we did.

I have absolutely no idea what went on out there, or the cause of it, and I sincerely hope that no one is in any serious trouble...but what I do know is that Will has been one of your most dedicated workers for as long as he's been doing this route. He's always smiling, always upbeat, and always efficient. We enjoy seeing him headed our way every morning, and we already know that we never have to check behind him. Just about everyone can tell that he loves what he does.

We hope that he (and everyone else) is okay, and we really would like to have him back as soon as possible, if that's possible.

Thank you for your time and attention, and if I can be of any further assistance on this matter, please do not hesitate to contact me.

Sincerely,

Lynne

"Wow, a character witness. Just that quickly, huh? You're right, that's unexpected." That brought a huge smile in the midst of major concern. "Man...you never know who's paying attention, and it's usually someone that you think couldn't care less. My wonderful customers...to the rescue."

"Aw, come on now. You know full well that the streets on Route 4 belong to Will Powers!" Chris said, sounding enthused about the possibilities.

"I try my hardest."

"But wait, there's more...", he said, "Even though mostly everyone had left the office by the time the whole ordeal got started, just about everyone defended your character in the midst of Emma's floor campaigning, and a lot of people came to me saying that they were willing to give written statements on your behalf."

"Seriously? Man...that's really touching. I mean, really...for people to not even know what kicked it off – well, with the exception of Hassan and Kim – or to not know the facts and to just believe in their minds and hearts that you're in the right." *...Sure hope they don't live to regret it later...*

"Man, listen", he explained, "Everyone around here knows you, they know your demeanor, and they know your character. We all think you're the nicest guy in the building. And of course, everyone is nice until you piss them off...but I don't think I've ever seen a fuse quite as long as yours. When Emma made her way over to me with her bullshit, I told her straight up that even if her story is 100% true, there's no doubt in my mind that she had it coming."

"No you didn't go there!" I said with laughter.

"Like hell I didn't. But speaking of Hassan and Kim…that's what I was getting to. Not only are they willing to speak on your behalf, but they actually got an earful of a conversation between management, right after you left Emma to watch your smoke."

"Oh, *really*?" I asked with raised eyebrows.

"AND not only are they willing to go on record testifying on your behalf, but they've already handed us written statements of just what they heard. We all know that time isn't on our side, so we have to make sure we're moving quicker than they are. Get this…"

[Emma walks back into the station in a huff, storms over to the supervisor's desk, picks up the phone and starts dialing a number]

Emma: *I know he heard me. I KNOW he heard me…*

Liz:*What happened? Heard you what?*

[Barbara walks out of her office and heads for the supervisor's desk]

Emma: *Heard me calling him! I was trying to tell him to leave the magazines for tomorrow and he wouldn't even acknowledge me.*

Liz:*Well even if he didn't say anything he probably won't deliver them. He's just mad right now. Let him burn it off...*

Emma: *Can't do that. He gave me some smart-alecky comment about only saving us fifteen minutes. He'll prove himself right even if he doesn't deliver them.*

Liz: *I thought you said he didn't acknowledge-*

Barbara:*What's going on?*

[Emma violently slams the phone down on the base]

Emma: *SHIT! He turned it off...*

Barbara: *Did you tell him not to deliver the magazines?*

Emma:*Yeah, I did...but he's not going to speed it up for us. If we don't take the extra off of him, I guarantee you he won't make the last truck. Then our asses are in hot water and having to explain all the way up to the district manager why he was out that late...*

Barbara: *I'll call him and tell him to bring the hour back.*

Emma: *Can't do that either. I just tried calling his cell phone, and it went straight to voicemail. I'm pretty sure he's turned it off.*

Barbara:*Well what should we do?*

Emma:*The only thing we can do; go find him, get the mail, and bring it back...*

Liz: *Or we could call someone whose phone is on, and tell them to go find him-*

Emma: …and work on getting his ass out of here while he's mad enough to incriminate himself.

[They all look at each other for a few seconds]

Barbara: Do you think you can manage it?

Liz: Oh come on! Is this really necessar-

Emma: Sure I can. He doesn't know his rights. None of these idiots do. I can take the hardball to a level he's never seen before. Only one thing though…I can't be there alone, because then that just reduces it to my word against his. I'll need a witness.

Barbara: That's fine. He should have been fired a long time ago. Liz, go with Emma. I'll hold down the phones while you're gone.

Liz: Um…okay.

Barbara: Call me when you're headed back here.

Emma: Will do! *[Gives a 'thumbs-up' signal, grabs her coat, and heads for the door. Liz follows her. Barbara heads back to her office]*

"Well I'll be damned", I said. "I thought that may have been what was going on, but I didn't tip my hand to Barbara. Hmmpf…and then she had the audacity to sit there in the office with a straight face and act as if she had nothing to do with it, and was trying to help me. Well, Holly and I knew that Emma and Liz's intent was to instigate, but I didn't know that they had been given a green light. They damn near were given an order."

"Well", Chris said, "It sounds like you got it together in the nick of time."

"No thanks to me, for sure. Thanks to even more unexpected help, and probably the most important piece of the puzzle. Susan."

"Susan?" Chris inquired.

"The rep that just happened to be there when I got back to the station after I was put off the clock", I stated. "I have very little doubt that my fate would have been etched in stone had she not been there when I got back."

"Are you sure she isn't an agent? I've never heard of her before now."

"She's not a rep for our craft. But she's definitely a rep."

"Oh, I gotcha now. Okay, glad she helped out, but don't hang your hat on that for very long. When representing clientele is what someone does for an entire area, after a while it all becomes a blur. Trust me; I work with her type all the time. I wouldn't be surprised if she's completely forgotten about the whole incident by now."

"Dude", I explained, "Not only was she with me from the second I stepped out of the truck, until about fifteen minutes before Holly showed up – and that was because she absolutely couldn't stay any longer – but she actually gave a written statement on my behalf. Signed it, left her contact number at the bottom…I mean, she treated the situation like I was the one she was there for."

"No shit?" Chris asked with genuine surprise.

"No shit. Be sure to ask Holly about that."

"No doubt. Usually people just pretend to care. She actually cared!"

"Those were my exact sentiments", I said with significance.

"Well speaking of written statements", Chris continued, "As soon as possible, I'm going to need you to revise yours. I read the one you submitted yesterday. It's good, but it's too vague. I'm going to need you to try your best to recall the entire incident, step by step…as much of it as you can remember."

"I can do that", I said.

"Good. You can send it to my personal email when you're finished."

"Okay, I think I still have you in my contacts folder. If I don't, I'll call or text you to get the address."

"Perfect", Chris said. "Okay, well I'm about to head into this building, so let me get off of this phone before they figure out who I'm talk-……hold…hold on just a second Will…"

Before I could say 'okay', Chris yelled out, "Man, WHAT?!" while he was still on the phone with me. There were a couple of seconds of silence, and then off into the distance, I heard a very loud "MEEEEEEE-HAAAAAAAW!" immediately followed by an even louder banging sound. I could tell that Chris was laughing, but it was one of those laughs that are so intense, you don't even make any sound while you're doing it.

"Don't tell me, let me guess...Hassan's stupid ass."

It took Chris a few seconds to regain his composure. "You already know", he said through his laughter.

"What was that noise I heard?"

"Him kicking the back of his truck", he said while losing his composure once again.

"I hope he re-injured his foot", I said facetiously.

"He knew which one to use. He's silly as hell, but he ain't crazy", Chris said after he got it back together, "But seriously though...man, keep your head up. I hate that it was you they targeted, and I hate that they were able to rile you up to the point that they could get you to stick yourself up like this, but we have the situation in hand."

"I sure hope so."

"We got it. Think positive."

"I'll do my best", I said as I tried to be reassuring.

"I'll be looking for that statement."

"No doubt. Right away."

"I'll see you soon...right here where you belong."

"See you soon."

"Later."

Chris hung up, and as the music resumed, I tried to process all of what I had just been informed of. Then I backed out of the parking space, pulled off of the lot, and continued on with the last leg of my trek home.

Two-faced bitch...

I backed into the driveway when I got home, in the hopes of mustering up enough inspiration to still go to the dance. I had to make certain that I was in the right frame of mind. I believed that you should go to a party to party at best, and to relax and shake off the problems of the world at worst. Lamenting about troubles just bores people...or so I thought. No complaining allowed. No one wants to listen to complaining...not even the ones that are paid to do something about complaints, but especially not the ones that aren't, and double especially not at a social event. But it had been a good day, as my parents and Chris had in fact been sounding boards for me to simply let them know what was happening. I was determined to let that be good enough. Still in all, it's hard to fake having a good time.

As I shut the front door behind me, I heard a melody coming from the basement. I headed down the stairs, and much to my surprise, the man cave had been taken hostage by what appeared to be the workings of Santa's elves. The coffee table had been moved out of the middle of the floor and to the side of the TV stand, and wrapping paper, rattan balls, ribbon, beads, crepe paper, and what looked like some branches from our trees in the backyard were strewn all over the floor. Denise was humming a tune, as she was finding a place for everything, while kneeling.

"What in the world is all this?" I asked.

Denise looked up and saw me. "Oh…Hi Honey. Renee's coming over and we're going to make ornaments for the tree. Wanna join us?"

"Oh, I am *definitely* going to the Bowl Ball now. Thanks for helping me seal that deal, Gorgeous. You do know, incidentally….that you can buy ornaments at the store, right? They're really not all that expensive, either."

"Now where's the fun in that? You're so commercialized."

"Call me commercialized and proud if 'traditional' means making ornaments from scratch like we live in a log cabin with no electricity or running water."

"I will, without hesitation. But…I am glad that you decided to go to the ball", she said with a smile.

I matched her smile. "And I'm glad to see that you're feeling better."

"Would you mind using the master bathroom, so as not to scare Renee in case she comes while you're getting ready?"

"Scare her?" I asked with a chuckle. Then I stopped and thought about it for a couple of seconds, and then struck a 'man of steel' pose. "On second thought baby, you're absolutely right…the poor girl might pass out if she gets a glimpse of me at the wrong angle."

The sound of her laughter was soothing to my conscience, and reminded me that things weren't so terrible. Losing my job would be painstaking, but would pale in comparison to losing any of my loved ones. Having this day to see them served as a reminder to not take them – or time – for granted, no matter what was going on in my life and no matter how pressing I thought any particular issue was. My pose had Denise keeled over, so I held it for a minute and grinned at her. When she gathered herself enough to straighten up, she asked, "Would you figure out what you're going to wear and get upstairs?"

"Your wish is my command!" I said right before pretending to take off and knocking the ceiling insulation out of place with my fist. As I embarrassingly repositioned it, Denise continued laughing at me.

The scene for the Bowl Ball was mesmerizing before I even made it onto the school grounds. Cars were everywhere, and people were streaming towards the school from all directions, after successfully hunting down a parking space. The staff was already redirecting overflow traffic onto the baseball fields behind the school, and the open field just south of the main campus. I chose the open field, which would fill up rapidly after my arrival. After walking the city block to get to the school and inside of the dance, my breath was taken away. I had heard that this was the one alumni event that I didn't want to miss, but it was almost unbelievable. It looked like half of the city was there! As I scanned the room, I almost immediately began seeing classmates, teachers, and school faculty members that I hadn't seen since high school, and others that I had seen since high school, but only on rare occasion, usually happenstance. The music had a 70's and 80's theme, and the sounds of Johnny "Guitar" Watson singing about inflation, depression, and being at the end of your rope were blaring through the huge speakers and echoing throughout the school halls. And everyone was genuinely happy to see everyone else. While people were definitely curious about what you had been up to in life after high school, no one cared about social status, or degrees, or what you drove to the party in or what was on your wrist. Everyone was just there for fellowship and a good time...to rekindle some old friendships, to laugh and reminisce about some old crushes, to act like high school seniors again, no matter our ages, and to celebrate being alive. And sometimes, that's a good enough reason to celebrate. It was just the escape I needed, just when I needed it. I socialized, I ate, I drank, I danced, and I forgot about all of life's troubles...with the exception of one recurring question and dim reminder. At least a half-dozen of my classmates all asked me, "Are you coming to the game tomorrow?"

And I gave them all the same answer: "Nah...I gotta work."

And my conscience gave me the same memorandum, each and every time...

No you don't, you lying bastard.

It ain't any fun playing charades with your life.

The Declaration

"It is always the best policy to tell the truth, unless of course you are an exceptionally good liar." — *Jerome K. Jerome*

December 17, 2010

Mr. William Powers
3767 S Mendenhall Rd
Memphis, TN 38115

Confirmation of Status:

William:

This is written confirmation of your emergency placement (without pay) effective Thursday, December 16, 2010, under the emergency procedures outlined in the national agreement.

A preliminary investigation has raised serious concerns about your misconduct while on duty Thursday, December 16, 2010. This action for emergency placement (without pay) is being taken because there is reason to believe your lack of restraint while on duty may result in your being vehement towards yourself or others.

You have the right to file a grievance under the arbitration procedure set forth in the national agreement within fourteen (14) days of your receipt of this notice.

Regards,

Barbara
Officer-In-Charge

Reviewing / Concurring Inspector – REF:

Despite my fun, energetic, memory-filled evening,

my mind couldn't stay wound down for long enough to let my body get anywhere near a full eight hours sleep, for the second consecutive night. It was more like half of that. I sprang out of bed in what seemed like the middle of the night, threw on my robe, unplugged my phone from the charger, and used the light from the screen to illuminate my path from the bedroom to the back door, while being careful not to wake Denise.

Our home was far from the newest or the biggest, but the location was unbeatable…nestled right into the corner of our subdivision in the Yorkshire Square neighborhood, less than 15 minutes away from both of our jobs by way of side streets, and only a couple of minutes from highway access. As I stepped out on my back porch, I could hear the Avron B. Fogelman Expressway and Bill Morris Parkway coming together in harmony before the break of dawn. I wondered where everyone's journey just beyond the privacy wall was leading them…and if I'd have no choice but to join them on a new journey of my own soon.

After a few minutes of taking in the brisk morning breeze, I went back inside and softly treaded to my home office. I pushed the door to, but not quite closed, as if to say "disturb if you must". Then I sat down in my desk chair, let the groove that my butt had worn into the seat pull me in, and began preparing my mind to do just what it wanted to do: tell the story the way it went. It was quiet, it was calm, and my memory was anxious to spill over onto the screen, in a descriptive fashion. I turned on my PC and opened up a new document.

I thought about exactly what I said, exactly what was said to me, and exactly the way I told the story to Mom yesterday morning…thoroughly. I began typing, and doing my best to bring the fine details of what a day's work entails when it's this close to Christmas day, and leave the impartial views out of what was being typed. I pleaded my case with the cold hard facts. That would be more than sufficient in clearing my name… right?

I completed my immediate task shortly after daybreak, after spell checking and double-proofreading. Then I saved my work, logged into my email account, composed a new message addressed to Chris, attached my newly revised statement to the message with pride, clicked on 'Send', and then shot Chris a text message:

"Check your email."

"Got it. Don't have access to a printer right now, but I'll read it on my phone when I get a break on the street."

"I'll be on the lookout for a response. Thanks for your help."

"No problem."

I had decided — actually, more like Denise had decided — that it would probably be a good idea to dust off the old job history and update my résumé as well. Just thinking about the possibility of having to return to the confinement and a cubicle and a desk job was enough to take the wind out of my sails. But I certainly wasn't about to put all of my eggs into recovering from this travesty. I pulled up my trusty document folder on my hard drive and opened up my résumé file. For a minute or two, all I could do was sit there, in the quiet of the morning, and stare at it while daydreaming about retracing my steps almost forty-eight hours ago, to ask myself what I could have said and done differently.

I had begun surfing the web to see what people with my educational background were taking home and how that compared to what I was currently making, when my phone started vibrating. I looked down to see who it was: Craig. One of the subs at my station who reminded me so much of me when I first started the job, it was almost frightening. We had taken to each other in sort of a big brother/little brother fashion. He had been to a few games of mine and my coworkers, he'd agreed to be a sub for one of the teams in our division, and he was considering joining our league as a full-fledged team member. Just then, I remembered Chris mentioning that he had done my route yesterday when we talked. I picked up the phone and pressed 'Answer'...

"What's up youngblood?"

"Oh, I was all prepared to get your voicemail... man, what the hell is going on?"

"I can't tell you anymore. You have to tell me. I'm on the outside looking in at this point."

"Okay, I'll tell you then. Some bullshit is going on. Some straight up bullshit."

I laughed. "I heard you were keeping my route warm for me."

"Among other parts of the city", he said. "Did Chris tell you about Lynne?"

"Oh yeah, the letter...yeah, he told me. When you get back there at the beginning of the week, be sure to let her know that I appreciate that."

"Without a doubt", he said. "Man! Just when I though I had seen it all...yesterday topped the craziest."

Let's see if I can be fazed... "What happened?"

"Well, after finishing up your route yesterday, I got sent back out to help another sub...one out of the latest batch. When I got out to the route to help her, I couldn't find her. Saw her truck, but looked all over and she wasn't anywhere she would possibly be while using that spot as a park point. Just as I was about to get frantic, she opens up the back door of the truck.

I asked her what she was doing, and she showed me a Tupperware bowl she was carrying around with her, right before re-wrapping it in aluminum foil. She was relieving herself...in the back of the truck. She was so intimidated and so afraid that she was going to face discipline from management if she didn't meet her deadline for street time, that she wouldn't even take a break to go use an actual bathroom. To make matters infinitely worse, there's a convenience store with decent bathrooms, right across the street from where we were."

"Well youngblood...I'd love to say that I'm surprised, but I'm not. Management is adept at threatening the newbies with termination."

"Don't I know it", he added. "And their definition of 'new' is damn near as warped as their definition of 'good'. They have the nerve to want to try and stick newbies with me so they can shadow me on the street. I let them know swiftly and decisively that I'd be more than happy to instruct just as soon as I received some benefits and not a minute before."

"There you go. Way to stand your ground. Don't let them put that type of responsibility on you. You're not certified or trained in doing that type of work, you're not getting paid for that type of work, and your attendance has been slacking anyway."

"Huh? My attendance has been slacking?"

"Hey, the latest word on the workroom floor, straight from the office hate campaign, is that your attendance has been slacking", I said as I smiled, but without breaking character.

"Well that would explain why you've been bamboozled, because between me being farmed out to the rest of the city, and you being on the street on most days before I even get on the clock, we hardly even see each other. And you know what else?"

"No, what?"

"It's some bullshit."

I laughed. "Touché."

"It's only a matter of time before you miss work when the only day you have free and clear most weeks is Sunday...the day where you can do the least in terms of taking care of business. It's not like we're doing anything different from what the regulars do on a daily basis, and we have families, business, activities and ailments to tend to as well. What is it about management that makes them think that 'substitute' equals 'robot'?"

"Management doesn't think anything", I said. "They're drones. They face north and receive irrelevant marching orders, then do a one-eighty and give irrelevant marching orders. Heard 'em once, heard 'em forever. You about to start?"

"Nope", he said aggressively. "They're still keeping

us off the clock for half the morning, and still telling us to be done and off the clock by five. Even with you out, and even with Christmas being a week away."

"And even with you knowing every route in the building better than half of the regulars", I added.

"Yeah, good old management", he said flatly.

"Believe it or not...that one there isn't really management's decision. It's in the local contract. You can put lots of things on management – and justifiably so – but that one there is on the home team."

"The union doesn't want us to start when the regulars start? Why? That doesn't make any sense."

"Not to a second-class citizen it doesn't. It makes plenty of sense to them...because they get to keep ensuring the regulars that more money will end up in their pockets, which keeps the memberships solid. You didn't know you were a second-class citizen?"

"Man, shut up", he said to the beat of my chuckling. "I'm about as sick of floating as humanly possible, and you got the nerve to be rubbing my face in it."

"You're right, my bad. I got much nerve calling someone a second-class citizen, from the chair I'm sitting in. I heard you did my route yesterday. Any of my customers ask about me?"

"Come on man...you already know. Not only do half the people that see me – or anybody else, for that matter – ask about you, but whenever I do your route, no less than two people mistake me for you. As of late, I tell all of them to just think of me as your younger, taller, far more handsome brother. I have to position myself properly so they can feel comfortable giving me all of the things they were going to give you for Christmas."

"You rat bastard you!" I said while impersonating a mobster.

He laughed. "Hey, we gotta get our benefits wherever we can. But seriously…I told most of them that you had a personal emergency. Don't know if I should've done that…it threw a couple of them into an anxiety attack. They all wanted you to know that they're with you."

I smiled inside. "No, that's fine. It's not like I wanted them to know the truth right now anyway. Wow, my customers…the best people in the world. I wonder if they'd still be with me if they knew the truth…"

"I'll bet the truth isn't anywhere near as bad as you think it is."

"Nah, it's pretty bad this time."

"It couldn't possibly be any worse than my truth. Man…when is someone in that place going to say 'enough is enough' and do right by the subs?"

"Probably never", I stated bluntly. "They have to have so many bodies that they can endlessly manipulate. You have at least two years before the current contract is up, and when it is, they'll come up with some new name for the same job that keeps you spinning your wheels."

"Never?! Come on now, they can't keep us in this holding pattern forever."

"Maybe not forever, but they can keep you in it for a lot longer than you think they can...a lot longer than you want to be in it, or should be in it." I paused for a moment. "Do you play tomorrow night?"

"I don't think my team is going to need me, but if you want me to show up so we can talk, I will. Germantown, right?"

"Right. But I tell you what...find out if your team will need you, and if they don't, then you can just meet me at the watering hole when I'm done. Only one thing, though..."

"What's that?" he asked.

"I'll need you to pick up the tab. I'm about to be broke pretty soon."

"Man, I'm already broke!" he exclaimed as we laughed in unison. "I gotta ship this Christmas package to my family so they get it in time."

"How is the family, by the way?" I asked.

"They're all fine. Clearly disappointed that I won't be able to get back there for the holidays for yet another year, but hey...the job's the job, and the job won't allow for it. It's extremely difficult to explain to someone on the outside just how it is for us. The only story anyone ever gets is the one of the regular and all the perks and benefits and how cushy his position is. They never seem to get wind of or pay attention to the other side."

"That's because the 'other side' isn't discernable to the untrained eye. They think everyone wearing the uniform is on the same playing field."

"You have a point. A very truthful point", he stated emphatically.

"Yeah, we'll talk in detail tomorrow."

"Okay. I may just swing by to catch your game."

"No problem. Whatever you decide, just let me know. Now get back to playing Hurry Up and Wait."

He laughed. "Of course. See you tomorrow."

"Later."

As I pressed 'End' on my phone, Denise pushed the door to my office open just enough to stick her head inside. She had a way of sleeping like a boulder when I was in the bed, and like a restless newborn when I was out of it. She probably had been waiting patiently for my phone call to end for at least five minutes.

"Good Morning", she said softly.

"Good Morning Love. No one's here but us."

"Shut up", she said with a scowl.

I beamed like a child. "Why do people keep telling me to shut up?"

"You're sitting here without a job to get up and go to, because of your mouth. Figure it out." It was her turn to beam.

"Hey, low blow!" I said with a scowl.

She twitched her nose at me. "I'm going to the Farmers' Market in a bit. You want me to fix you some breakfast before I go?"

"Nah, I'll grab some cereal. Don't worry about me."

"You sure?"

"I'm sure."

"Making good on your promise to update your résumé?"

"I was about to tackle that in a bit. Right now I'm searching for naughty pictures on the internet." Her lips curled up into a snarl.

"No, seriously…I just finished revising my statement of yesterday's events. Chris told me that the one I gave yesterday wasn't detailed enough. I'm sure he's right…I was too wound up, my thought process was too crooked, and things were happening too fast for me to think of everything after they got me back to the office."

"So they'll let you override the statement you already turned in?" Denise asked, sounding puzzled.

I shrugged my shoulders. "I guess so. I'm sure that Chris wouldn't ask me to go through the trouble of reworking it if he knew it'd be inadmissible. I already sent it off to him, but I may not hear from him until late afternoon. He has to work."

"Understood. Well, I see you're busy, so I'll leave you alone", she said before puckering her lips and then smiling. I matched her endearing gestures.

"See you later. Love you."

"Love you too."

She pulled the door back to the position it was in before she stuck her head in it, and went on her way. I opened up a new tab on the internet and began pulling up all of my old career profile accounts from various job websites to update my résumé, in preparation for the worst. I then began looking through job listings... only to discover that the openings in the current market were on the disappointing side of things. The only thing I hated worse than changing jobs was changing homes...especially when there was a very good element about the job I had that made me want to hang onto it. But at that moment, I couldn't figure out if what I liked about the job was worth the fight that I'd inevitably face.

I decided at that moment to push it all aside to make way for eating cereal in the man cave, while watching the college bowl game previews and festivities on ESPN...without any nagging from Denise. Sweet Liberty!

∽

I had gone from sitting on the couch to being stretched out on the couch, and from watching the New Mexico Bowl to the New Mexico Bowl watching me, when I was awakened by my phone ringing. I reached over while still flat on my back and picked it up to see that it was Chris. I pressed 'Answer' as I sat up straight…

"Hello?"

"Hey Will, what's up?"

"Not much", I said with a yawn. "Just sneaking in a catnap."

"Oh, my bad. Sorry to wake you."

"Oh no, if anyone in the world has the right to wake me up, it's you. I take it you got a chance to read the statement."

"I did, and I also ran it past Holly. We're definitely going to have to go over this and make some changes."

"What's wrong with it?" I asked.

"Well….now, in comparison to the one you gave after you got back from the street, this one is *too* detailed. The people that are going to read your take on what happened need to get to the meat and potatoes of the matter, before it gets too bogged down. If it's too long before they get to what we really need them to read, they're going to put it down. We don't want them to put it down."

"Okay, that makes sense…thorough, but without all the fine details."

"Right, exactly."

"Okay, what else?"

"Well…" he said before a short pause, "you can't have it sounding like you were angry."

Huh? But I was angry… "Oh…I can't?"

"No man. We have to have something to work with, and we need to try our best to look as if you weren't the aggressor out there."

"Then shouldn't the point of contention from our side start with the fact that I left them where they were standing at the station in order to avoid an argument?" I asked. "Someone yelled at me, I yelled back. I mean, they were the aggressors before I left, and there were a whole lot of dominoes that fell before it actually got to a point of me being the aggressor, even on the street."

"Yeah, but…we gotta try to make it sound like you weren't ever the aggressor throughout the entire ordeal", he explained.

"Hmmm…" I had to stop and think about that one for a few seconds. Because I knew what he was asking for, and it immediately didn't sit well with my conscience.

"If we don't, then I can hang it up, huh?"

"Yeah, man…you have it sounding like you were

ready to dole out some knuckle sandwiches right there on the spot."

"Actually, it was more like some hoof sandwiches…but I hear what you're saying."

He laughed really hard. And while I was listening to his laughter, I felt a wall that my mind had put up come tumbling down. I began to figure that it really was okay to laugh about the ordeal, because it's only human nature to try and make the best out of a bad situation, and rarely—if ever—is one's mood stagnant. You're usually headed towards whatever mood you happen to find yourself in, long before you actually get there. And if I wasn't headed towards happiness, then I'd definitely be headed towards depression… or rage. So mixing honesty with humor and keeping it moving in the direction of happiness seemed to be what I naturally wanted to do…so I just let it flow. I realized at that moment that it's quite possible for something to be both serious and funny at the same time.

Now, if I could have just wrapped my mind around the concept of all of this damn dishonesty. Just as I was coming to grips with that dim reality, here comes Chris hitting me with the latest dilemma. How in the world was I supposed to make it appear as if I wasn't mad, without turning the entire scene into a complete fabrication? Some evidence had already surfaced that would prove anger on their side of the coin, and some completely unexpected support on my behalf had come into play that could lead one to conclude that I was upset. But the most damning element of them all was what couldn't be gotten around...my own words. Threatening to kick someone like they just branded your thigh isn't something that you do when you're calm and collected, let alone nice and accommodating.

"Come on man...be serious", Chris said after getting his afternoon laugh out into the atmosphere.

"Okay, okay...being serious. I'll try my best, but I don't know just what I can promise you with this one. I'm not a very good liar."

"Lying is such a harsh word", he said sort of jokingly. "You don't have to lie, but you do have to be something of a wordsmith. You just have to come up with creative ways to sort of bend and finagle the truth...sort of."

"Wow...", I said, "...so even with all that led up to me posing a threat, I still have to remain dignified all the way through, huh?"

"You *have* to", he said with conviction.

"Okay. I'll look my statement over, and trim the fat, and take all of the emotion out of it. I'll try to have a revised statement to you no later than lunchtime tomorrow."

"Sounds good," he said. "We gotta get you back in here a.s.a.p."

"And that sounds good to me", I responded.

"Alright man, I'll talk to you tomorrow", he said, sounding as if he had picked up on my disappointment.

"Tomorrow it is. Later."

"Later."

I pressed 'End' on my phone, and after it hung up, it showed me that I had one unread text message. It was Denise, letting me know that she would be visiting family after she was finished at the market. I replied and told her that I loved her and would see her when she got home.

I put the phone down on the coffee table, and let out a sigh. So for my own clarification, now I had to figure out if the fight in front of me was worth fighting, and I knew for certain that I couldn't fight it my way.

I got up from the couch and went back upstairs to my home office, where my résumé was still on my computer screen, waiting patiently. I minimized it and opened up the file of my revised statement – the factually accurate one – that I had worked my butt off to get completed first thing in the morning, and was deathly proud of myself for submitting. I didn't want to change it. I wanted to take my chances with what was.

I sat down in my chair, and resigned to spending the rest of the afternoon taking what I felt was a truthful masterpiece, and turning it into something I didn't even recognize myself when I was finished. And after reading it back to myself…it was something that made me seem bland, robotic, devoid of emotion, and incapable of fending off this onslaught brought on by people out for blood. I made myself into the wooden dummy I felt like…with someone else's hand up my backside, pulling the strings and mouthing my words for me. A coward. Before I had even completed it, I felt a little piece of me dying.

I can't believe I'm actually doing this. Why can't we just roll with the facts? What's so hard to understand about every action having a reaction? So what if one side is the so-called "boss"? No one's going to believe this shit…

I saved my work, composed a new email message, attached my re-revised statement to the message, clicked 'Send', and sent Chris another text message. He confirmed shortly thereafter. I looked down at the corner of my computer screen to check the time.

4:26 PM

I opened up the internet and began bookmarking job postings on my saved websites, for positions that

I thought I might have any chance of landing, with little promise to be found. The future was bleak...

Then...I stopped. I rolled over to my file cabinet, went into the bottom drawer, and grabbed my special key. I got up and walked back into our bedroom, and got down on my hands and knees beside the bed. I reached underneath and slid my custom-made case out from under the bed frame, and used my special key to unlock it. After I lifted the lid, I straddled over it before sitting down on the bed, turning the case to face me. As I looked down, I contemplated.

And then, as the rippled waves of red overcame my vision...the thoughts started sinking in. Thoughts that I lived too blessed of a life for and really should have been ashamed to admit I had, yet fed the evil gene that was embedded within my soul. The sight of high powered ammunition that had been set free from a barrel, on a collision course with human skin and muscle tissue. The sound of a metal cylinder connecting with a jawbone, complete with teeth flying in several directions. Someone with blurry vision, lying flat on their back, staring at the bottom of a boot coming down on their face repeatedly and forcefully, before losing consciousness. A skull cracking. Ribs breaking. A spine being repositioned. Desperate gasps for air. Retaliation. Vindication. Blood. Carnage. Hysteria. Destruction. Death...

Something snapped me out of it, as I shook my head. My eyes remained focused downward, as I gave a cold, hard stare to what looked like blind ferocity taking the place of what fleeting hope remained within me...

The Machine

*"No man means all he says, and yet very few say all
they mean, for words are slippery and thought is vis-
cous."— Henry Adams*

I always liked when my league game was in Germantown. There was a popular sports bar near the corner of Winchester and Riverdale Bend, where a few
of the guys from the job and the league would go to
have a few drinks after our games. They had great late
night bottle beer specials and a great waitress: Sherry.
She'd always take care of us when we ventured away
from beer and went for the stronger stuff. Usually we
would have two or three tables pushed together because there'd be so many of us, and we'd be sending
up a cheer for the victory, and setting up all of the
emptied bottles and glasses in the formation of bowl-
ing pins. But on this night, four chairs at one table was

three too many for starters, and in the beginning I'd be drowning all of my sorrows. I had a terrible game... good only on the boards. Almost a dozen rebounds, but only a couple of blocks, a couple of assists, no baskets from the floor, and four missed free throws in the fourth quarter. We lost by six points. Felt as if I let my team down. I'm big on focus, and tough on anything that I see as a distraction. And to call this job ordeal a distraction would be the understatement of the century. I felt like I played the entire game with a leaf blower strapped to my back. I felt like just going home, but I had promised Craig that I'd have a drink with him after the game.

I sat at our usual table near the bar in Sherry's section, fiddling with my phone...and all the while figuratively kicking myself for not having the presence of mind to use it when it counted the most, to even up the score. The worst part about me behaving the way I did was that I saw Emma and Liz coming from a good distance away, and I knew it was them even before I saw that it was them. Had I been thinking straight, the thing to do in that situation would have been to grab my phone, cue up the video recorder, begin recording them before they even stopped the van to get out, and then conduct an interview. "Hey, what are you two doing here?" That probably would have stopped them dead in their tracks. Maybe not when it came down to putting me off of the clock, but at least then not only would I have had an eyewitness to confirm my story, it would have been one that's guaranteed to never lie. Better judged by twelve than carried by six. I was always doing something or another with my phone… why couldn't I have thought of it then?

Because people that are out of their minds from anger don't make intelligent choices…DUMBASS…

"Hey you, where's the crew?"

Sherry sort of startled me. I was so mired in my thoughts, that I wasn't even paying attention. She was standing right over me, rocking back and forth on her heels and toes, and twirling a tray in front of her. She'd probably been looking at me for a bit and knew I was contemplating something and immediately tried to lift my spirits.

"Oh, hey…I think they all went home. Not much to celebrate tonight. Or maybe they just didn't want to be around me…can't say that I blame them."

"Well there's always next week", she said in a bubbly tone. "Wanna get started with the usual?"

"Actually, there is supposed to be one more person coming. I'm a little early, so I'll wait for him to get started with the usual. I'll personally get started with a double shot of Rémy Martin."

"A *double* shot?" she asked. "Don't you have to work in the morning?"

Eh, boy... "Yeah, that's why I need a double."

She laughed. "Place is still crazy, huh?"

"You've no idea", I said as I made eye contact and shook my head.

She shrugged her shoulders. "One double shot of Rémy, coming up! Ready, set...tab!" With that she succeeded in getting a laugh out of me.

As she scooted off to put in my order and I began reaching for my wallet, my phone rang. I thought that it might be Denise checking up on me, but actually it was Nick, a friend that Chris, Hassan and I knew from league, and also a colleague out at the Bartlett station. *Here we go again...* I pressed 'Answer' on my phone.

"What's up Nick?"

"Hey man, nobody's supposed to see the bottom of your shoes unless we're on the basketball court. Don't be an abuser, man. That's not how we were raised."

"Eeee-vrybody's got jokes", I said as I opened up my wallet with one hand to try to scoop out a credit card.

He laughed. "How are you doing, brother?"

"I'm doing, is all I can say right now. I'll know how I'm doing in about a week."

"I hear that they put you off the clock."

"Yep. Not exactly the way that you'd like to get some time off, but for me it seemed like the only way. I'll take it for what it's worth, except for the fighting-to-clear-my-name-from-the-outside   part. Humph…I just said that like I have a choice in the matter."

"Have you thought about filing a lawsuit?"

"A lawsuit?" That one gripped me for a moment. "No, I haven't. For what?"

"Harassment, disparity in treatment, and discrimination. We have legal reps for our side in matters like this. I can help you with the paperwork, if you want me to."

Sherry saw that I was on the phone, so she set my double shot down in front of me. I held up a credit card for her, and she took it and kept it moving. A double shot at this establishment was like four shots anywhere else, and with the bomb that Nick had just dropped in my lap, her timing was impeccable.

"Ooh, that sounds awfully heavy. You think this situation is worthy of a lawsuit?"

"From your position, what harm can it do?"

"Well…I'm thinking it could do quite a bit of harm when it's time for another company to hire me", I said as I quietly put the glass up to my lips to take a sip of my shot while listening.

"Nah, information like that rarely gets disclosed between companies unless they ask for it on an application, or the case is so huge that it ends up going mainstream. But please tell me you aren't going to just throw in the towel that easily. Oh, and by the way…have you called Andre yet?"

I knew this question was coming… "No, I haven't talked to him yet."

"Why not?"

"I actually thought I'd see him at the rec center. I got there a little early to catch his team's game even if he didn't play. But he wasn't there…must be out of town or something." *Stop lying.* "I kinda feel like calling him makes me look like I'm guilty and trying to gain favor. You know he's on the court team, right?"

"Of course I know!" Nick shot back. "That's exactly why you need to call him. Never mind that he basically got you in the door for the gig, he thinks the world of you, and in some ways looks at you like a son. And never mind that you know he's not going to call you."

I took another sip of my cognac as I searched for a response.

"This ain't the time for pride, brother", Nick said. "Do you have any idea of what their account of the events that took place is going to sound like?"

"Actually, I kinda do", I said to the rhythm of his beat. "Their report has it sounding like I was the Hulk out there stomping on Strawberry Shortcake. But even worse, I got it from the grapevine that the boss had it in for me all along. I don't think I'm supposed to know, but I do."

"Oh, the union's working with you?"

"Trying to", I said as I set my glass down.

"Who's the boss over there now?"

"Barbara."

"That clown? Man, now you *really* have to square up and fight with everything you've got. Do you know what her problem is with you?"

"I'm Andre's boy?" I asked hesitantly.

"Well yeah", he said through a short laugh, "But it's deeper than that. Much deeper. Did you know that I actually did a little supervisor stint at your station?"

"No, I didn't", I said.

"Well it's really neither here nor there, but I was the one that actually replaced her on the first go-round. She actually was under Andre when she was trying to sleep her way up the ladder."

"No shit?" I said with mild shock.

"Yep. In addition to her advances being dismissed like she had just told a stale joke, toward the end of Andre's term as boss over there, she pulled some shit that's eerily similar to what Emma and Liz pulled on you. She called herself conducting a surprise street inspection on someone who told her that he was overburdened on that particular day. She rolled up on him on the street while he was eating his lunch and tried to tell him he had no right to be taking a lunch break without authorization, and she did it completely behind Andre's back. Her wannabe-ass got put in check quickly. Not only did she lose her desk job, but she got busted back down to street level *and* shipped out to the rural station."

"Oh shit", I said with surprise. "That's where I remember running into her when she was our craft! It must've been the humbling stage of her career."

"I'm sure it was", Nick continued, "because she had to whore herself out to every middle manager in the entire district just to get off of the street and back to the metro again. Not even her family ties could save her from that demotion. So she's making up for lost time…"

"Hmmm…I always wondered how some people not only seemed to transition from craft to management without as much as a crease, but move up the ladder so quickly. Damn…when it all went down, I actually was still enough of an optimist to believe somewhere deep down inside that we might actually be able to stick together on this one."

"Well it has very little to do with breaks. If it isn't about arrangements and 'favors', then more often than not it's about middle management testing you to see if you're willing to be their personal lap dog. I had to find that out the hard way. And when I did, I hurried up and got back to the street. When Barbara applied for a supervisor position and got her first little taste of power under Andre, she tried to make "sticking together" take on a whole new meaning." I laughed at that one.

"So of course she has to fuck with you", Nick explained. "She can't say or do the things to the person that actually helped to create her status in the first place, and self-reflection is a fantasy…so she's picking on the little man. In her mind, getting at you is the same as getting back at Andre."

"Yuck", I said as I expressed myself in a way that mimicked the first and only time I tasted beets.

"What's wrong?" Nick asked.

"I just pictured some of the guys that I know by face in middle management. And then I got a visual. Man…now it's actually starting to make a little more sense to me. Of course I'd already heard about the slut reputation through the rumor mill, but I keep my head down and my mouth shut when I'm at work. I wonder how her husband copes with that shit…"

"Hey, some men prefer slutty women", he claimed.

"Well more power to them", I replied. "Man, what some women won't do to stay on the cutesy side of operations…"

"It ain't who you know, it's who you blow!" Nick said as I smirked. "And that's why I hurried up and got my ass back to the street. My heart and mind wants to show people the respect I want to be shown. But actually making your way into a permanent desk position on actual work ethic, and nothing more? Please. You're either a man and sucking up, or you're a woman and, well…just sucking. Or…you have a connection within a connection, which is the needle in the haystack. But it is why so many women are on the cutesy side of operations. Because that's exactly where they can use what they got to get what they want. Especially the ones that were drunk off of power to begin with. They get that first little taste, and from that moment…for some, it's like being high on cocaine…"

"And who better to have in charge than a bunch of ball busters, if you want to pattern your business after a boot camp, but you're stuck in the private sector", I added. "Even though we can be some supreme assholes ourselves, men automatically know that even being the boss isn't going to save you if you cross a certain line with the wrong man. On the other hand, no matter how much she might deserve it…there is absolutely nothing to be gained from kicking the shit out of a woman, except universal shame and the permanent brand of "abuser." And they know it. So they get to ratchet up their assholish-ness to a level that's higher than most men."

Nick let out a 'good guy' laugh, as he repeated "assholish-ness" to himself.

"But maybe keeping quiet is part of your problem,

Will. That's how things build up, and you end up exploding. Sometimes you just gotta come out of the corner and go toe-to-toe. Not physically, but verbally... beat them to death with their own rules, you know? You can't get weary in the fight to not have your name and reputation dragged through the mud...because management is relentless."

"Nick...at this point, that's exactly what it's all about for me; not exploding", I said as I shook my head. "When you realize you're working with a bucket that has a hole in it, it's useless to continue to try and put water in it. There's only so many ways you can say the same damn thing. And I've figured out all one-hundred-and-one of them. There's nothing left to say. I keep my head down and my mouth shut not for them, but for me. Eleven years, man...eleven fucking years. And the only thing that changes is whose mouth it's coming out of. They're purposely obtuse, and I no longer have the capacity to deal with that. If any of them talk to me for a little too long, I'm going to snap. My wife and family deserve better than that, but I can feel it..."

"You know, I never even thought about it that way before", he said, "...but you're onto something." Then he cleared his throat. "Look man...I'm not trying to ruin your evening, but it's not going to take long for things to start piling up on the home front, when nothing's coming in and everything's going out. You're going to have to try and recoup this pay that you're losing right now...if you get back. IF you get back. Maybe I shouldn't make it sound macabre, but if we've already heard about what happened all over the floor in my station, then you know what you're facing... right?"

"Yeah."

He hesitated, as if he didn't really wanted to say what needed to be said.

"Letter of removal."

"Yeah."

Sherry eased back over to the table to check on me. As I looked up to make eye contact with her, I noticed Craig coming through the front door. I used my free hand to give Sherry a 'thumbs up', right before waving Craig down.

"This is your job, man. A good job..." Nick stated emphatically. "You gotta utilize every single option available at this point. Who cares what it looks like you're trying to do?"

"I hear you man, don't think I don't", I said glumly as I refocused. "It's just been kind of overwhelming with trying to get everything in order at this point, and with all that's going on in real time with the family." *You're still lying...*

I picked up my shot, smoothly took about half of it down, and let the burn settle in my chest cavity.

"Well I don't think either one of us wants to know what 'overwhelming' is really all about, so think about what I said, and let me know if you want to make a move on that. But don't take too long…there's not a huge window of opportunity here. And find some time within that real time to dial that number and do what you have to do."

Craig had scooted himself into the seat directly across from me, and Sherry was already greeting him. He saw that I was on the phone, so he let me wrap up my conversation.

"Will do. Thanks for calling, and thanks for your concern. Seriously", I expressed to Nick.

"No problem. We got you on the schedule next week. Prepare your ass for this mule kicking I got waiting on you."

"And on that note, I'm hanging up in your ear. Goodbye clown."

He laughed. "Catch you later." I pressed 'End' on my phone.

"What's up old timer? How are you making it?" Craig asked as he extended his hand.

"Oh, I'm making it as well as can be expected, given the circumstances", I said as I reached to give him a brotherly handshake.

"What's that?" He asked while pointing to my glass.

"Cognac. Want a shot?"

"Uh, no..." he said while grimacing. "I can smell that all way over here. I'm perfectly fine with beer. Bring on the late night special!"

"Suit yourself", I said as I picked up the glass. "Far be it from me to argue a man's poison." Craig nodded in agreement.

Sherry came over to the table and set two beers down. Craig had ordered for us while I was on the phone with Nick. I raised my glass with what remained of my shot high over my head.

"To drones!"

He raised his beer bottle to meet my glass. "To drones!"

As beer bottle met glass in the air, nearby patrons probably thought we were some sort of military nuts. I took the rest of my shot to the head, and he knocked off about a third of his beer. I exhaled, let the burn in my chest rekindle, closed my eyes, and smiled. Craig's cheeks expanded, as he realized he'd taken in too much too fast, and he had to take his time getting it all down. After he'd swallowed just in time to catch his breath and cleared his throat, he acted on his eagerness.

"So, as I was saying yesterday morning...when are we going to cross over? Hasn't this hazing bit gone on long enough?"

"Man", I said, "...do you really want to get into that?"

"I think I've been there plenty long enough, passed initiation, put up with enough crap, been as accommodating as humanly possible, and proven myself more than enough times to be in a position to ask to be treated fairly", he answered. "And if I'm totally honest with myself...I'm tired of playing Mr. Nice Guy. Management thinks that the way to run a business and instill morale into their employees is by coddling whoever squeals the loudest, and acting as if everyone else in the place is blind. Maybe it's time for me to start squealing."

"I have an even better idea", I said. "Maybe it's time for you to brush off that résumé, update it, and try to find yourself a job that will put that degree to good use. What did you say your degree was in again?"

"Information Systems..."

"Man, why in the world-"

"It's boring", he said as he cut me off. "I know that the tech field is the boom, yeah, there's good money in it, but...I don't wanna be cooped up in a server room all day every day. I like fresh air, and the great outdoors. I like solitude...the kind you just can't get when so many others look to you for solutions to problems with their company computers. I had to learn that the hard way. With this job, I can turn it into a physical challenge and stay in shape without a gym membership. I can check out all of the neighborhoods and tell myself which house I'd own if I lived on this side of town. I can soak in a little bit of nature, as I watch seasons change. I can figure out which one of your customers I'm going to be like the most when I get older...and the money here is just as good! I mean, it is once I make it to your level..."

I sat back and listened to him as he spoke on how he felt. *Very introspective. A lot like you were when you were at the same point in your career. Are you sure you want to do what you're thinking of doing?*"

He continued on. "...I can delve into my thoughts and meditate on the problems of the world. I can blast my tunes, or listen to talk radio, or sports radio...I can run through fields in the summer, and make snow angels in the winter...much to the humor of customers. It's worth it. Yeah, you have to deal with all kinds of bullshit when you're in the office, but when you get out of there, it's worth it. If you never let go of the kid in you, then it's kind of like getting paid to relive all of your grade school recesses all over again, each day. And this holding pattern they have us in won't last forever. I'm confident it won't. Pretty soon I'll have my own..."

"Man listen", I said, "I already told you about the contractual obligations, right?"

"Right, you did."

"Okay, so even if they wanted to do something with you guys before then, they couldn't. But I guarantee you they don't want to. It'd be different if I actually saw some light at the end of the tunnel, but it's getting bad, man. It's getting bad. Remember Michael Jackson's song in The Wiz?"

"Huh?"

"Nevermind. And plus, if that day ever did come, you probably wouldn't make the cut anyway…seeing as how your performance ain't making the grade."

"Huh??? What do you mean, 'performance ain't making the grade'??"

"Yeah, man. On top of you calling in sick every other day, the hate campaign team has been all over the floor, spreading how your performance of late has been seriously slipping. Every day – when you DO actually decide to bring your ass to work – you're out there parked in front of the donut shop, with your feet kicked up on the dashboard, taking half-hour breaks, and working unauthorized overtime…like you're a regular or something. You were good when you started…really good…but you just ain't cutting it anymore…or so I've heard."

Craig glared at me. I looked right at him, threw my hands up, and smiled.

"Hey, don't shoot the messenger. I'm just telling

you what I've heard. I didn't say that I've seen any of this myself..."

"You haven't. Know why?" he asked.

"Why?"

He put his palms on the table and used them to push himself up out of his chair. Then he leaned forward, to the point where his nose was almost touching my nose.

"Because it's some BULLSHIT!"

As a few patrons looked around to make sure they didn't need to be on guard for a bar room brawl, I cracked up.

"My performance hasn't gone anywhere but up since the day I set foot into that God-forsaken office", he said while easing his hind quarters back into his chair. "I take my ass to work, I absorb as much as I can, and no matter how much they may try to insinuate the contrary, there will be no Jedi mind tricks taking place here. The reason why you get wind of it is because the minute anyone steps outside of their little imaginary boundaries, they construct witch hunts, in an attempt to get and keep us at each other's throats. They indirectly and directly tell me that I suck, and whisper into everyone else's ear that I suck, while simultaneously giving me all of the assignments that you have to be a seasoned veteran in order to complete in the time that they want you to complete them. It's bullshit...a way to create animosity, especially between the haves and have-nots. Of course I see through it…as you can see", he said with a shrug, "…but I haven't quite figured out if they're real witches yet."

"Wow, look who's paying attention!" I said while laughing. "Let me help you with that last one… they're witches. They're well-trained and well-versed in using your own emotions against you, and they're given free reign. And that's why the only way to cope and navigate your way through these waters is with your brain. You can't lose control. I lost control. And now look where I'm sitting. This is the end result when they succeed in watering the seed planted in your mind that tells you to get all the money you can get while the getting is good, which leads you to defy your intelligence and your body for the sake of making their numbers look good. They'll have you out on the street hobbling around with a damn broken ankle, convinced that you're not tough enough if you simply want to do what any injured person's mind is signaling them to do: seek some medical attention."

"That's why I think it's time to start squealing", he explained. "The one damn time when I literally was sick since I've been doing this job was when I had a wisdom tooth erupt on me. Tried to be nice, tried to work with them, tried to do things the right way. Called the place, Liz picked up, and I told her that I'd be calling in the next day, so that I could keep my dentist appointment to have the tooth removed. Know what she had the nerve to ask me?"

"What?" I asked.

"'Is it going to take all day?'"

"Get out!" I said with an enthusiastic sarcasm that he didn't pick up on.

"No bullshit", he answered. "It was one of those moments when you wish you were at complete liberty to say exactly what you're feeling. Because I wanted to say, I don't give a damn if it's going to take fifteen minutes! You won't be seeing me tomorrow, and I'll bring you the dentist's bill for proof WHEN I get back!"

Craig was animated and humorous in his reenactments of conversations with our superiors. And he was succeeding in lifting my spirits...along with the beer and cognac.

"I think that their default mechanism is to think that everything you tell them is a lie, because everything that they tell you is a lie", he stated.

"Figured 'em out, huh?" I asked as I took a swig of beer.

"Not only have I figured them out, but the pain in my ass via the pain in my mouth is nothing compared to Eddie."

"The pain in your *ass* via the pain in your *mouth*?

See, I knew you were from Wyoming. You told me you were from Alabama."

"You motherf-"

"ANYWAY..." I said as I interrupted his onslaught with a grin, "Who's Eddie?"

"The new guy that didn't even last three weeks. He was on his way to work when his mother called to tell him that his father had just suffered a heart attack and was being rushed to the hospital. He called the station to let someone know what was going on, got Barbara. She asked him the same question that Liz asked me, and when he let her know in no uncertain terms that that question was highly insulting, she had the audacity to tell him to bring proof to substantiate his claim...as if someone on probation wouldn't already know to do that with a family emergency. No empathy, no compassion, no nothing. Numbers. Well, at about three that afternoon, his father died. He called Barbara back to ask her if that was proof enough...right before calling her every breed of bitch there is under the sun. And of course, decided not to return."

"Oh wow...I was wondering what happened to him", I pondered. "I never even knew what his name was before now."

"We had exchanged numbers and talked a few times", Craig said. "I guided him to a few hard-to-find locations on the street." I genuinely felt bad for the guy, and didn't have the heart to try and persuade him to do any differently after his loss. I haven't been there that long relatively speaking, but I've been there long enough to know that incidents like that leave a bad taste that never completely goes away...especially when they start talking to you afterwards. They want you to take the attitude that they're just doing their jobs, and all you can think about is how shady they were acting when they wanted something done. In a way, I sort of envied the ones with the gumption to leave and never look back. To everyone on the outside looking in, they're dumb. I personally think it's smart to take hints quickly when your gut is telling you that you aren't built for this. With some people, you don't have an infinite number of times to hold termination over their heads as ransom for their lives, and on top of only caring about numbers, management loves threatening you with your livelihood. Every little tiny infraction ends with the sentence, "I sure would hate to see you lose your job."

"Well, you handled your situation the right way, and the new guy is...was...all the proof you need for that one", I said. "If you know your ass is covered, then don't waste your breath trying to explain anything to them. But seriously...it is good to think your way through what you would have said and done if you had the leeway to say and do it. It's a great tension release.

And all the people that are supposed to be representing you would say upon hearing something like that is 'don't let them intimidate you like that'...as if, after all that you've experienced firsthand and all that you've witnessed, the confidence to not let management intimidate you just fell out of the sky and landed on your head. You subs are actually smart enough to know what's headed your way if you try to buck up against management. You know that where the rubber meets the road, you're on an island. If you're on the bottom, you're not guaranteed a career, and as such, you're not an equal in their eyes. Meanwhile, if you're at the top, you can mow a 90-year old pedestrian down and they'll have you back in the driver's seat in three days. Too many in our craft at the top have been there for too long and simply can't realize that the place has changed drastically for the worse...because none of the changes affect them."

"Hey hey hey, someone who's paying attention that doesn't really have to pay attention!" Craig exclaimed. "But ultimately, you know that at the end of the day, no matter how much they pound the hell out of you guys, you really only have to take so much and then you can tell them all to kiss it. It's not so easy with us, especially when you're uninsured and don't really want to create a hospital bill anyway. I had to pay for that tooth extraction out of my pocket.

And it's pure mercy that I haven't suffered any type of real illness or injury for all this time that I've been uninsured. But hell, even when the opportunity to just get off of your feet and lay down for a while would work wonders, they try to make you feel like the devil's spawn for even letting that thought enter your brain. "Walk it off." That's their favorite line if you call to let them know you're hurt. Twisted your ankle in a rabbit hole? "Walk it off." Fell down a flight of porch steps? "Walk it off." Charmin took a chunk out of your left ass cheek? "Walk it off."

He caught me with that last line just as I was taking a swallow of beer, and while I caught myself before the spit take, he did succeed in choking the hell out of me. While I was coughing uncontrollably and other patrons were now wondering whether or not someone was going to have to perform the Heimlich maneuver, he got out his chair and began patting me on the back, while laughing his ass off. I used one arm to shield the cough and the other to push his arm away from my back. When I was finally able to lift my head, my eyes were filled with tears. Despite blurred vision, I could see every tooth in his head through a stupid grin. "You okay?" he asked, proud of his accomplishment.

"Yeah, no thanks to you!" I said as I wiped my eyes.

"My bad. Well, not really", he beamed. "But yeah,

as I was saying…you know what the crazy part is? All we want is the same thing you have…some security, some benefits, and some peace of mind. Did we do something wrong?"

"Yes", I replied. "You didn't start when we started. Never mind that you were probably still sleeping in a crib at night when we started…you missed the boat. Their living is made, damn you. And face it, young-blood…for as long as you stay, there's nowhere to turn. You're a number. A rented mule. A guinea pig. A disposable ink pen. So just remember…there's no in-centive for excelling and dedication, and until they feel like doing something other than testing out their nutty little science projects on you, forget about freedom of speech, take that bass out of your voice, and take that broomstick up your rectum."

If I could have seen my face when I was watching Denise roll around on the floor laughing after I told her the events of that fateful December day, I would guess that it probably looked exactly the way Craig's face looked at that moment. As I leaned back and clasped my hands together, I knew that the truth serum had taken hold. So I didn't fight it.

"Look…at least once in your life, you've probably turned on the news, or picked up a newspaper, or surfed the web, and heard or read about an episode of workplace violence where somebody with less intestinal fortitude went crazy behind this shit, and you wondered why. Well…now you *know* why. First of all, don't sweat any of that 'lose your job' talk. If you show up every day on time, put forth an effort, and don't do anything incredibly stupid, you're as good as gold. And they know it. All of that 'lose your job' talk is just one of a bunch of intimidation tactics designed with keeping you productive, and keeping your mind off of everything that someone doing the same identical job is getting and you aren't getting. In most companies, the cream rises to the top. In ours, the sludge rises to the top. Everybody's trying to play the role of hard-ass so they can work their way up through the ranks…or at worst, not be demoted to having to do something they're incapable of. Those who can, do. Those who can't, supervise. The end result is people that are as dumb as a box of rocks directing the ship. And the only motivational tool that someone as dumb as a box of rocks has, is fear."

My vision was momentarily impaired by Sherry's arms, placing two fresh beers in front of us. She could tell that we were discussing some pretty heavy things, so she didn't say anything and kept it moving.

"Had I known you beforehand, or had you been a relative or a friend of mine", I said, "I would've told you to think long and hard about getting into this. There's really no hope for *us*, so what chance in hell's kitchen do any of you all have?! It's a game...a shit-stained game. They sold you a bridge, youngblood. If someone tells you that you have a chance to win this game, then...wonderful, I guess. And if whoever tells you that is actually putting some legwork behind their words? Well that's superb. But when they're finished talking and they walk away, make absolutely certain to tell yourself that your end of the stick will be shorter than a coffee stirrer. Then, when that's exactly what happens, you won't be disappointed. And be sure to thank me later", I said as I grabbed the fresh bottle and put it up to my lips. After taking a big swallow, I saw that he was still in receiving mode. I set the bottle down on the table convincingly.

"I would recommend absolutely nothing short of you getting out while there's still time to preserve your mental well-being," I said. "You don't deserve the shit they have in store for you. The concept of how a business is supposed to be run is completely turned on its head at our job. Management pretty much does what they damn well please in the name of achieving numbers...which wouldn't be entirely bad, if they weren't totally clueless. You can expect them to try to run the place with a sense of ethics, fairness and balance, but that's an expectation you'll be taking to your grave with you. They're little more than glorified babysitters, so their plan pretty much consists of the road that has the least amount of tantrums on it. And then, of course, you gotta look out for their 'favorites'. The clear-cut company policies that they'll persistently persuade you to violate are the same policies that they'll nail you to the wall for violating the very second that it's convenient for them...while one of their 'favorites' is completely in the habit of violating policy, and intentionally being overlooked. They reward the hard workers with more work, and the union ensures that a place will forever be set at the table for the fuck-ups, so no room on the platform will ever be cleared for the up-and-coming hard workers. Like you said, you can't even get a couple of hours to rest your body after taking a serious tumble, or a simple day off to keep a medical appointment, let alone a stretch of days or a week for a vacation, so your body never gets enough time to properly rest and replenish itself, and your mind never gets enough time to properly flush all of the garbage that the place feeds it. You're cramming more work into less time, and unable to leave for family emergencies, make family functions, etcetera...while you're looking right at us – and management – skip out of the door after eight hours to do those very things all the time. They push you, and push you, and push you, and push you, and push you, until finally, they find your breaking point. Their *problem* is, they don't know what someone's going

GODFREY WILSON III

to do after they break. Someone might go home and cry in their cereal, while someone else might go grab some high-powered automatic weaponry and start extracting pounds of flesh. And the people that are supposed to be doing their best to protect you at every turn could give less than a damn for as long as they aren't the ones in management's crosshairs. Some of them actually like watching the low man on the totem pole get treated like a second-class citizen. Meanwhile, you got regulars out here abandoning company vehicles – with work left to do – to go shopping, go to brunch, go to sleep, get laid, get drunk, get high, get haircuts and manicures…on company time…"

As I put my beer up to my lips while watching Craig deflate right in front of me, I had all of the empathy in the world for him, because I know just how gung-ho someone can be at the thought of the possibilities. But my conscience ate at me every single time I knew for a fact that he – or any of the other newbies, for that matter – was operating with misinformation. And he liked me. He looked up to me and my work ethic. I couldn't run the risk of having him upset with me for not being truthful with him when the opportunity arose.

He rose his head up out of his funk to make eye contact with me, as the corners of his mouth formed a grin.

"Can't win, can't break even-"

I interrupted him by holding up my index finger, to buy enough time to swallow what I had just taken in.

"But you can...get out of the game. Some can't, but YOU...can. You're not so deep into this doo-doo that you still can't make a break for it."

He looked at me seriously. I locked into his eye contact.

"And you *need* to get out of it. There's nothing for you in that place, youngblood. You have a college education, you have common sense, you have streets smarts, but most importantly, you have a heart and a soul. All while you're growing up and trying to make the right life choices, you hear, "Go into such-and-such field, they make good money!" The money's here, the money's there, the money's over there, money money money money money. So you spend the best years of your life chasing money, then you get a little older – like me – and you come to realize that money ain't shit. Not in the sense that you don't need money to survive and thrive, because you do...but all of the money in the world doesn't drown a miserable set of circumstances. And for as long as you all don't have what we have, the money just balances out. Go after stability... you're never going to get it here, let alone some normalcy and peace of mind. You're too far down on the totem pole. Even if you have to take a step backwards in money right now, it'll pay off in the long run if you can get with a good company. I know young people like to live life on the edge, and believe that they're invincible, but you can only live without a net for so long. And in the meantime, think about charting your own course and being your own boss. It's getting harder and harder to sustain middle-class status with just a j-o-b. Companies aren't interested in taking care of employees and families like they used to. It's almost to the point where you *have* to have a side hustle..."

"I hear you," he said. "I really do."

"But are you listening?" I asked.

He struck a pose of contemplation as Sherry set another beer down in front of me. Mine was almost empty, his was almost full. She'd only brought one this time. She was attentive, from a distance. I looked up and made eye contact with her. She winked. I refocused on Craig while I knew I was getting through to him.

"Man...go out into this world and do great things", I ordered. "Money in exchange for your health, sanity, and balance just isn't a good trade-off; and you'll still never make the money you deserve. You all have been stripped to the bare bone, to the point where the only thing good about the job is the paycheck. And it's only a matter of time before they begin to compromise our position as well. You're too good for this, and you're way too good for them. They don't deserve the likes of you. Do what you love. Yeah, this is cool, but there's a glass ceiling involved that certain people don't want you know about. Chart you own path...one without limitations. If you wanna go to the brink of insanity, then fine. But make sure someone else isn't pushing you there. I didn't do that, and that's why I'm in the position I'm in right now. You still listening?"

"I am, really", he stated flatly while raising his eyes up from the table. "Might not seem like it...but that's only because I was trying to keep hope alive."

"Well if you have a decade or so to devote to hope, then stay put. But I know you're better than that."

He folded his hands and rested his chin on his thumbs, as he placed his elbows on the table. I moved the bottles in front of me to the side to make some room for my forearms. I could sense that he was beginning to meet me where I was...and I could also sense that my speech was becoming a little bit slurred.

"Go home...get closer to family", I said. "Don't take for granted that they'll always be here. Cherish this time, and cherish the relationships with those that care about you. And in the meantime, look for a company that appreciates intelligence, dedication, and loyalty... because all of that will just end up being squandered here. When something doesn't make sense to you, a red flag is *supposed* to pop up…that's the way that the human brain is designed and hardwired to work. It's what keeps us from entering into potentially dangerous situations in life. Don't ever teach yourself to turn off your intelligence, for anything or anyone."

I picked up my new refill with the glee of an Irishman, while it seemed as if Craig was now all of a sudden trying to figure me out. I think that my speech may have been confusing due to all the truth serum, which I'm sure was dilating my pupils at this point. I gulped down almost half of the fresh, cold bottle in my hand as if I had no doubt that more alcohol was the cure.

"Meh…enough about my bleak future", he said as he sat back and attempted to relax. "Tell me something old timer", he asked as he stroked his sparse chin hairs, "…how is it that a man can be so revered by the customers he serves and at the same time so despised by the people he reports to? I mean, you know that I eventually get around to every block in the area. And no one — and I do mean *no one* — even comes close to being appreciated and respected as highly as you are. Everyone on your route knows you. The elders know you, the kids know you…hell, the dogs know you. You say something bad about Will Powers to anyone who lives on route 4 and you got to kick somebody's ass… or take an ass kicking!"

That was a rare 'feel-good' moment throughout

this bout of turbulence. All I ever wanted was to be the best at anything I ever set out to do in life, and of course the job was no exception. Respect was important to me. I burped and smiled. He laughed.

"And of course", he continued, "I can't be anything but a silent observer whilst I'm in the midst, lest I redirect the bloodhounds' attention towards me...and until I let your advice soak in and feel comfortable in knowing that I can seek out gainful employment in this economy, we can't have that kind of thing going on. So what gives?" he asked with a shrug.

"First of all, that 'old timer' shit is going to be the death of you", I said while pointing at his nose, as he smirked. "Second of all", I said as I put my beer down and leaned back again, "To answer your question... they're pretty much one and the same. I'm smart, and I don't kiss ass...with of course, my wife being the exception." I reached for the bottle, as he made a gesture with his wrists that resembled a convict in shackles. I glared at him, while he kept smirking.

I shook my head and got back to explaining. "Our customers are easily noticed, smart, and observant. And I've been holding that route down for long enough to watch kids that I first met when they were barely out of elementary school - aiming their toy guns at me and inviting me to join their Barbie doll tea parties - grow up to receive Bar Mitzvahs and graduate from high school...many of which I've gotten invitations to."

"I noticed!" He said emphatically. "What *else* on your route have you gotten invited to witness??" The smirk had reappeared and was rapidly transforming into an evil grin.

"Man, shut up and listen to me..." I didn't know if that last line was me speaking to him or all of the truth serum speaking to me. "Listen youngblood, seriously...nothing can compare to the connections you make in a neighborhood like mine. You're up close and personal with everyone..."

"I've learned that", he interrupted while nodding. "I worked your route yesterday too. I *really* don't know what to tell anyone now...other than it's nothing tragic. They're genuinely worried about you. Not only do your customers know your days off better than us, but they also know that it couldn't be a vacation...because you wouldn't go on one without giving them a heads-up."

"Let's *hope* it's nothing tragic", I said matter-of-factly.

"You know they aren't going to fire you over this", he said. "If they can get away with this shit here, it truly will be tragic. Let you tell it, Emma and Liz were acting like *they* were the damn police. Who the hell do they think they are to go out to somebody's route and take something off of you like they were going to do the work themselves within the hour? The union has got to go after that with everything they have."

I clutched the neck of my beer bottle like it owed me money. "Well don't fool yourself into thinking for one minute that this is going to blow over lightly", I told him. "They got the goods this time around, and they're going for the jergula-......the jerkula-......the juckula-......They're going for my neck."

Craig shook his head at me.

"I'm not the union's whipping boy per se, but it's something about actually believing in a day's work for a day's pay that doesn't jibe well with our local. Nobody likes a curve buster, and nobody gives a damn about what they're supposed to give a damn about. Everyone from the very top to the very bottom is just milking the cow for all they can get until the cow dies. And when that happens, they'll cut the cow up and sell it for beef."

"I really do hate to hear that", he said, looking like a student full of empathy for his favorite teacher. We both paused for a second.

I shook my head again, set my bottle down on the table and released my death grip, and sat back. "Anyway, where was I? Oh yeah...my philosophy is quite simple: show people the respect you'd like to be shown. Give respect, get respect. I feel as if I give more than ample respect, and that's before anyone even gets the chance to show me that they don't deserve any. Management, on the other hand, thinks that they deserve respect because of the chairs they're sitting in. And as such, they get what they deserve…shit."

Craig laughed at me.

"There isn't a single person in our station that isn't on the "favorites" list with anything that remotely resembles a spine, that wouldn't let off some choice words if they knew it wouldn't cost them in the long run. If I knew it wouldn't cost me, I'd make it my daily mission in life to hurt their feelings, just on a general principality."

"Okay, that did it", Craig said. "I can't sit here and listen to your drunk, depressing ass for any longer." Then he rose up out of his chair, made eye contact and said with a grin, "Seriously…I gotta get some rest. I heard an ugly rumor that they're finally going to abandon this stupid 'no office work' rule for us. So I'm probably going to be awakened from a very deep, alcohol-induced sleep by a phone call telling me to come in early. We're closing in on the big day, volume is simply too high, and they can't enforce the rule without getting into serious trouble with the area manager, due to people being out well into the evening."

"Well ain't that some shit", I said as I shook my head slowly. "All I had to do was wait a couple more days – or be someone other than who I am – and saying I'd be

FORWARD TIME EXPIRED

out 'til 8:00 would have been understood perfectly. I hate my life."

"Man…are you okay?" Craig asked as he looked down at me. "Seriously. Are you going to be able to make it home safe?"

I looked up at him for a couple of seconds, pretending to be stern.

"I'm…wonderful! I don't have to get up in the morning for a damn thing! Ain't that wonderful?"

"Whatever", he said as he grabbed his jacket and began to put it on. "Shoot me a text to let me know you made it home safe. When you get back to work, don't forget to quit moving your ad magazines to someone else's case so the newbies have to work them two days in a row."

"Ha HAAA!" I replied. "I don't do that, but as soon as you make Employee of the Month, I'll tell who does to stop."

"You know what, Will? You can kiss my bright, sunshiny ass."

"No thanks, I'm not a switch hitter", I said with the same stupid grin he had on his face while I was choking. "Go get your ass kissed in Wyoming. I kiss my wife's ass, in every sense of the phrase, thank you very much. Pay my tab, scab."

"Wash some dishes, old timer", he said while waving his arm to summon Sherry. "Gotta go empty out the bladder and hunt down this waitress of ours. You sure you're good?"

"Yeah, I'm good. Thanks for coming out to check on an old timer", I said as I slipped out of my chair to stand up, which required a little more concentration and balance than I expected. I tried to conceal the results of my overindulgence.

"Never a problem", he said as he smiled and extended his hand. We gave each other a goodbye shake, and then exchanged a brotherly hug. As he headed in the direction of the bathrooms, I looked up at the huge plasma TV in the corner of the bar to catch a glimpse of the Sunday night game that was holding most of the bar patrons on the edge of their seats. It was a barn burner. I tried to stop the TV from drifting to the right of my peripheral vision, but couldn't quite manage. I stuck my hands into my pockets and tilted my head back to stabilize myself.

The visiting team was trying to pull off an upset with their backup quarterback. Just as it looked like they were about to crack the red zone on the way to the winning touchdown, the home team made a drive-stopping quarterback sack. It was then that I realized that I hadn't caught a single play of the game before that one, despite being a football fan, in a sports bar. Most of the patrons let out a huge cheer for that play. I just stared at the screen, motionless and emotionless, hoping that it would become motionless as well. Motion denied. Then, while seemingly everyone in the place was anticipating the next play, I looked down at the empty shot glass and all of the empty beer bottles on the table, and my phone sitting next to them.

I felt a tap on my left arm. I looked around.

"Are you sure you're alright?" Sherry asked with genuine sincerity and curiosity. I looked down at my phone, sitting on the table. I ran my finger across the screen. Then my eyes focused on the floor.

"Yeah…I'm alright." *…being sober in a bar is against the rules…*

"You haven't had too much to drink, have you?"

Yes… "Only in the sense that my bladder is over the hill."

She laughed. "Yeah, you're okay. Craig already took care of the tab. Go home and treat that lady of yours right", she beamed as she handed me my credit card before switching away.

"Always!" I blurted out as I threw up the peace sign for her. She turned her head and winked at me, before strutting into the kitchen area.

I reached over and grabbed my jacket off the back of the chair, and put it on with a flinging motion that made me lose my balance and stumble a couple of steps to the left. More cheers erupted from the bar patrons. As I regained my positioning, I slipped my credit card into my jacket pocket, as trying to put it back into its proper place at that moment would have required entirely too much concentration. I looked down at my phone again. I picked it up and stared into it, like I was waiting for a solution to this mess I was in to pop up on the dark, blank screen. I thought maybe if I turned it over and shook it like those big 8-ball toys we had way back when we were kids, when I turned it back over, my answer would then be crystal clear. But alas, I wasn't a kid anymore. Nothing was staring back at me except for a blurry reflection.

I slid the phone into my jacket pocket and attempted to head for the door in a straight line.

The Battle

"Those who can make you believe absurdities, can make you commit atrocities."—Voltaire

I was really, really bad at calling people back. When it was a call I never wanted to make in the first place, I was even worse.

deep breath, deep exhale…

{{{Several rings}}}

"Hello, this is Andre. I'm unable to answer your call right now…I'm somewhere enjoying life. So leave a message after the beep and I'll get back with ya…if you're worthy. Ha Ha. Later…"

:::BEEP:::

"Hey Dre...it's Will. Do you remember when we saw each other at the gym a couple of weeks ago and you asked me if I had been fired yet, and I told you that I was waiting for you to come back and do it? Well, I guess I couldn't wait any longer. I figured I better call you to give you the scoop before you started hearing it from the wrong people and places. Call me back."

I pressed 'End' on my phone, and then checked it to see what I had missed throughout the night. A couple of interactive games where it was my turn to play, a voicemail message from Pop wanting to know if I had heard anything yet, and a "Home safe" text message to Craig that I had no idea I had sent. Nothing from the job to be found.

I plunked my phone onto the coffee table, let out a sigh and a grunt, and stretched back out on my leather couch – where I'd laid down when I made it home from my stupor the night before. Still fully clothed, taking only my jacket and shoes off, so as not to bother my wife, and just in case I had to jump up in the middle of the night to puke. The couch was one of my few possessions that I actually kept from my old bachelor pad. It had a perfect place in our new basement, it was long enough to hold me when I did decide to stretch out, and it still pulled me right into the groove I had worn into it when I laid down. It always soothed me after a hard day's work. But with days gone by and no work to be had amidst the holiday season, there wasn't much comfort to be found anywhere. I clasped my fingers behind my head, and scanned the room with my eyes. Denise had done a great job decorating and arranging everything...the pictures of us, all of my basketball memorabilia & posters, the wall art from my apartment that she actually liked, the dart board, my college degree...she was adamant about me having a man cave, and I was adamant about not getting in her way on this one. And just like that – in one stupid moment of indecision – I threw all of her hard work into jeopardy. My heart wasn't ashamed of my actions, but my head was admonishing my very existence. I actually was hoping that Andre had picked up because hearing from him at that moment would've helped in sobering me up. But I couldn't even catch a break in that area. *We can't lose this house. We just got it. You've never gone backwards financially in your entire life. You can't let your wife down. You can't let your family down. You can't let yourself down. Where's the fight in you, for heaven's sake...*

Denise came downstairs, looking a lot like Christmas. Typically there were no classes the week between Christmas and New Year's Day, so the entire school staff had that week off, but it was Denise's personal custom to take vacation time the week before Christmas as well, so she had the last two weeks of the year off. She flipped the light switch to 'on', and when she did, the light was like a lemon would have been to my taste buds, as I squinted and squirmed and reached over to the coffee table to feel around for my glasses without looking. She walked over to the table and handed them to me.

"Good morning Love. A drunk ain't shit."

"Don't I know it", I said as I put on my glasses and palmed my forehead. "What time is it?"

"Nine-thirty", she answered. "And you better be damn glad that I can sleep through a hurricane, or else I would've been upset about you not coming to bed last night. I missed your feet when I woke up this morning."

"Just didn't wanna bother you, that's all", I said as I shielded my eyes from the light as if it were the sun. "Wasn't sure I'd be able to make it through the night without sounding like a caveman had invaded the master bathroom." I tried to find a spot on the ceiling that would let me know if my head was still spinning.

She laughed as she looked down at me. "I'm going to Wolfchase Mall to wrap up my shopping. Wanna come with me? The mall is usually good for helping you get into the Christmas spirit. We can do lunch afterwards...I was thinking about hitting the Blues Café on Beale Street. They've got the gumbo that you love the most! I'm treating!"

I looked up at her and found a quick smile. "Nah, I think I'll just lie here for . . . . . .for a couple of weeks." I refocused on the ceiling.

"Aw, quit with the moping, would you?" she said with her hands placed firmly on her hips and her weight shifted to one leg. I couldn't bring myself to pretend to be in the mood for anything that involved spending money, because I wasn't as sure as everyone around me that this ordeal would blow over shortly and everything would be back to normal soon. I was already gearing myself up for 'rainy day' mode, while simultaneously working carefully to not throw those I cared for the most into a panic.

I forced myself to smile at her. "Nah, you go on and have fun. The way I'm feeling right now, I'd just be the proverbial turd in the punch bowl. . .for you and everyone else at the mall."

"That is such a gross visual."

"It's supposed to be."

She slapped her thighs and let out a sigh, and then she gently sat down next to my outstretched body on what little space there was on the couch, and began rubbing my stomach, which had been growing rapidly ever since I had gotten the chance to sample her cooking on a regular basis.

"Baby…" she said with a look of comfort, "…we're going to get through this. It's just a temporary setback. Just stay positive, and we'll break through. If it's money you're worried about, then don't be. Yes, I know the holidays are upon us, I know that it gets tight around this time, but I'm going to hold us up until you get back…even if that means that when you get back, you're working somewhere else. I personally don't think it'll happen if the story went the way you told it to me…but if it does, I'm not worried. You had a job before this one, and you'll have a job after this one. They can't keep a good man down – and especially not the one I believe in."

"You mean all of that, Love?" I asked sincerely, with a slight grin.

"Of course I mean it!" she exclaimed. "All relationships hit rough patches, and it's not like the treatment you've been receiving on the job is a mystery to me. I'm your sounding board, remember? But anyway…I said at that altar that I'm in it for better or for worse, and I meant it. There's no 'cut and run' in me."

My grin turned into a huge smile. "Now how could I possibly turn you down after such a reinforcing pep talk? Let's go to the mall."

"You're so sweet", she said as she gave me that coy little smile that I remember drawing me in like a vacuum, the first time we met.

"Give me time to shower and change."

"Done deal."

As Denise headed for the stairs, I put my feet on the floor and got up off of the couch, only to realize that I had stood up a little too quickly. "Whoa…"

Denise stopped and turned around. "You okay Baby?"

I winced right before looking over at her. "Do we have any Sprite?"

She laughed again. "I'll see if we have any in the garage, but I think we're out."

"Thanks Love."

As I headed for the bathroom in the basement, Denise yelled out as she trotted up the stairs.

"Ain't shit!"

I shot a look in her direction, but she was already at the top of the stairs. I held out my arms like a tight-rope walker and made it to the bathroom to turn on the shower.

***

"Two dollars and seventy-five cents for a twenty ounce soda!" I blurted out as I got into a showdown with the vending machine. "Am I hung over or hallucinating?! Should've stopped at Conoco!"

"You're at the mall, cheapskate", Denise rang out. "Now would you *shut up* and just buy the freaking soda?"

"Quick, give me some money", I said as I gestured to Denise with my hand without releasing my stare at the price tag.

"Oh, no you don't", she quickly countered. "Any other time I'd be the loving, accommodating wife that I am and buy it for you. Trying to settle your stomach? You're on your own. Next time don't drink so much."

"You're not the boss of me!" I retorted with a quick turn of the neck. Then I broke character and smiled, as I could see that my objective had been completed... a snarled lip. Then, as we shared a laugh together, I reached into my pocket and peeled off three bucks.

Wolfchase Mall was bananas. It looked like there was a sign over the main entrance that said "Everything's a Dollar!" That's how many people were there. Online shopping was supposed to be the big boom and the new 'in' thing, but you couldn't prove it on that day. People still loved the hustle and bustle the holidays brought. Not to mention the mall experience... something that shopping at home was simply no match for. The mammoth Christmas tree, the holiday decorations, the young children waiting in line with their parents to give Saint Nick their wishes while the one on his lap was freaking out, the new cars that you had a chance to win in sweepstakes drawings, the charity gift wrappers...it all blended together to make a fitting portrait. I was amazed at just how many people didn't have to be at work...because I know they all couldn't have gotten time off the way I did...

But at the moment, I honestly didn't care all that much for a job. As necessary as it was and as much as I wanted to be assured that the service the good people on my route had grown accustomed to wasn't being forsaken...I chose to live in the moment and simply pretend as if I had the good life that those around me appeared to be taking in. Denise and I were having an outing. I genuinely enjoyed the time we spent together, and both our public and private chemistry. Getting my ass up and off of that couch was just what I needed, and she knew it. We both had gotten so bogged down with our work schedules, extra curricular activities and hobbies, trying to squeeze togetherness and quality time onto the calendar had become just another chore. On most days the evening routine was Denise keeping dinner warm so that I could inhale it right before showering and getting some sleep, so that we'd be prepared for the next day, to keep the finances flowing and the household running smoothly. We weren't about glamour and glitz or keeping up with the Joneses; that's simply what it took in this day and age to keep the ship afloat. So we didn't get many opportunities to do what we were doing. I had done more in the name of spending time with family in the last three days than I had done in the previous three months. And

I was sick and tired of neglecting everything and everyone, for not being able to make time. It never took much to please me, and I was having fun. Every time I went to the mall, it felt like my very first time all over again…I just had to make my way to it.

Denise was really into the shopping, and I was more or less along for the ride, as we bounced in and out of just about every store in succession, collaborating on gift ideas. We were rummaging through the clearance section in the rear of Gap Kids when I felt my phone begin to buzz on my hip. I grabbed it to see who it was…Andre. *And away we go…*

"Hey Love, I have to take this."

"Sure Honey, go ahead."

"I'll text you to get your location when I'm done", I said as I headed out of the store.

"Okay, no problem", she said as her eyes followed me out of the store. I pressed 'Answer' on my phone as I kept walking.

"Yell-low."

"Where the hell are you?" Andre asked cynically.

I looked to my left and my right, to find a place to talk that wouldn't feel to me like I was infringing upon others' space.

"At the mental hospital, waiting patiently for my assigned rubber room."

"You know what? That even beats my idea of going

to the animal farm to rent a mule. Based on the statements I read, that might seriously help your cause at this point."

"Couldn't possibly hurt it..." I said as I spotted a 'Restrooms' sign. It took a couple of seconds for what Andre had just said to sink in.

"You read my statements? Where'd you get them from?"

"Where do you think I got them from? I got them from Chris! Yours *and* theirs! And now all I need is what's in the middle. So tell me...what the hell happened?"

"Wait a minute...you already got both sides of the story in the form of our statements, and you weren't going to call me to let me know that?" I asked as I started walking in the direction of the sign.

"Aw, that's no fun," Andre said, as I could hear his grin through the phone. "If I called to let you know that, then you may not have gotten the opportunity to squirm. But back to what I read from you...sounds fishy. So what gives?"

I made it to the sign and saw that it was a long hallway with a convincing echo, and the restrooms were nested at the very end. I walked halfway down and plugged my free ear with my finger.

"What you read from me wasn't my idea. It's a bunch of lying by omission, and I'm not a very good liar." *I'm learning though...regrettably...* "But I was told that it was my best chance. I had prepared a second statement that was as thorough and as truthful as I could make it, and that one also includes what was discussed when we got back to the office. But I was told that statement was too detailed, and if it doesn't get to the point much faster, the team's just going to put it down."

"I knew that statement I read from you wasn't your idea", Andre said. "You're too honest for your own good. Especially as it pertains to refusing to play the game how management wants it to be played...and having the nerve to tell people that you report to just what it is you think of them...although you have gotten much better with that over the years. I was more curious as to why the union told you to go that route, because in this particular case, the team might actually be more interested in what you aren't saying than what you are saying. And what's going to...oh...and we didn't have this conversation...right?"

"What conversation?" I asked.

"Perfect. What's going to make the people on the team put a statement down is if they smell bullshit on it. The truth is your best defense."

"Well the truth is what I wanted to tell all along", I said, "But the union doesn't think that's a good idea."

"I can't lie and say that my advice would be any

different if I was union and trying to direct your steps. But your problem is, everyone in this business knows everyone else, and news spreads like wildfire. Emma's coughing fits make you think she's about to keel over right there on the spot, she can't see straight, and you'd think she did two tours in Saigon by the way she acts. You're tall, fit, athletic, and young enough to be her son...damn near her grandson. No one on the team is going to believe that Emma's half-dead ass had you crying for your mother out there. They're going to believe what I believe – if they're objective – which is what you're telling me...the two of you butted heads. If they're not objective, they're going to believe that Emma thought she was about to die...which is probably what would've happened if you had kicked her teeth out, in mule fashion."

"Is the team objective?" I asked.

"Not really. But unlike the nitwits that you report to on the floor, it isn't because they've gotten a little piece of authority and gone ape shit with it. It's because they've been trained to be robotic as it pertains to getting to the heart of the matter. And the heart of this matter is your threat, and the nature of it."

"That's sort of what I figured. But my mind and my heart told me to plead my case anyway."

"Guilty with an explanation, is still guilty," he exclaimed. "Your best bet is to throw yourself on the mercy of the court. Just tell 'em something to the tune of, 'hey, look...I snapped. I was having a bad morning, the wife was on my back about the bills, I'm under a lot of stress..."

But that isn't the truth either! Not you too, man... I moved the phone away from my ear and let the sound of his voice fade into Wah-Wah Land, while letting out a heavy sigh. Heavy sighs had become the soundtrack for my life. After about ten seconds, I put the phone back up to my ear.

"...must've blacked out or something, and it all just built up to one great big explosion. The work load was just the straw that broke the camel's back.'"

"Okay, okay, I got it." It was becoming increasingly tougher to mask my frustration. What I had to keep in mind though, was that everyone was just saying and doing what they believed would help.

"What's the matter, big guy? You sound like your resolve is worn thin, and the fight's just beginning." Andre had detected my frustration over the phone. "This isn't some elaborate house-husband scheme you got going on, is it? Denise doesn't strike me as the type to carry a man", he said with a laugh.

"You're crazy...you know that, right? But you're correct about two things...my resolve has definitely worn thin, and I am under a lot stress." *Just not for the reasons you want me to throw out into the atmosphere.*

"I'm really and truly beginning to wonder if all of this is worth it."

"Is it worth what? Your job? Your job that you gave up white collar America for, because you could kick the desk to the curb and still stay in a middle class tax bracket? Is it worth *that*?" He asked seriously.

"Yes, *that*", I said seriously. "My intention was never to neglect anything and everything outside of work. I'm no longer balanced and haven't been for a while now, no matter how hard I try or how well I hide it from the rest of the world. And right now, I just don't know where this job is going, but I do know just what it's slowly but surely eroding me into. All morning long you hear managers blurting out demands to get to your workspace and cut out the chatter. I rarely if ever leave my workspace, and I rarely if ever chat with anyone about anything. So I'm doing what they claim they want done, and they *still* manage to find their way to me every morning. You're not doing this right, you didn't do that right, we're not seeing all this time you claim you need, so we're not approving any of it…and I have to admit, I don't think I can take much more of it. My head's not right, man. I'm constantly and consistently thinking about things that are horrible and demonic, and taking great pleasure in those thoughts. Every morning when these supervisors come around with their crap, I can literally feel my blood start to boil. I can't even respond to any of it without getting the shakes. I know everything in life has its tradeoffs, but I'm not built for micromanagement…especially when I know it's all based on false information and lies. At least with a desk job, I could be left alone."

"Man, they aren't doing a damn thing to you that every manager in the country isn't doing to every single worker on the floor, and lying is the foundation of Management 101", Andre rebutted. "It's the culture of the business. Take your ass to the gym before work and pretend that the heavy bag is whoever you feel like knocking the hell out of that day. I guarantee you, your blood pressure will regulate. But whatever you do, don't just give up and join the ranks of the unemployed – especially in this economy – because the job you currently have could be better."

"'The culture of the business'? See, that's exactly what I'm talking about. That's what everyone says… 'They fuck with everybody.' Why am I the only one that sees something wrong with that picture? They're not supposed to be fucking with anybody! They're supposed to be conducting themselves like professional adults. How come no one expects more?"

"Okay, okay, you got me", Andre surrendered. "I don't know why it has to be the way it is. This isn't the culture that I manufactured, this is the culture that I was given. And I think that no one in your craft expects more because everyone knows just how people end up in management to begin with. Just be glad that you got in on the right side of the closing door. Because if you think your position is fucked up, then you don't even wanna begin to fathom just how fucked up it's going to be for everyone behind you. At least you're getting paid to put up with the bullshit. Everyone behind your group of hires and on down isn't, and they never will be."

"Well, this turn of events has caused me to delve into some serious introspection, and when I think about all of the things that I don't want to be, unemployed is number five on the list…below irreparably sick, certifiably insane, incarcerated, and dead…all the things that no amount of money can bring you back from. The energy put on the workers from the people in charge is all negative and all flows in one direction. When the people you work for make it their mission in life to drain you in every way possible, eventually you're going to end up drained. It's just a matter of time."

"Well, it sounds to me like you've given up."

"Not given up, just put things in the proper perspective. No matter what approach I take, I kinda think my fate's already been decided."

"No, no, not even close. You just have to play it right", he said. "And I don't think anyone working with you on this believes that your fate has already been decided. I sure as hell haven't. Of course you know the current people in charge are going for the pink slip, and because that's what they want I'm sure that by now the area manager has gotten word of all this shit...but my hat is still in the ring, and I can use my influence to sway the crowd in your favor, so long as I play it right just the same. The rest is going to be up to you to decide. The game is what's on the table; our only option is to play it. Man...never a dull moment..."

"You know Dre", I said, interrupting his contemplation, "I have to be honest. I really didn't want to bother you with this. So don't put too much thought into it, okay? I'll be fine either way."

"I know you'll be fine either way, but that doesn't mean that I'm going to stand idle and watch you get steamrolled by anyone whose very intention all along was to put you in the position that you're in..."

He paused for a few seconds.

"Do you still have the revised statement you gave? Not the one you gave on the spot, or the one I've seen...the one I *haven't* seen. The one that says what really was going on out there."

"Yeah, I still have it", I said apprehensively, somewhere in between a question mark and an exclamation point. Andre paused again.

"Email it to me."

"Man, are you absolutely sure you're not getti-"

"Yes. I'm sure."

It was my turn to pause.

"Okay. I have to be on my PC to attach the file, so as soon as I get home, I'll get it to you."

"Gotcha. I'll be on the lookout for it. Your case will be coming up in the next day or so, because I know that no one wants to drag this out over the holidays. So get that to me as quickly as you can, and don't make this an easy decision for anyone. And for the love of God, don't kick any civilians between then and now."

"Man, shut up." I smiled, and even though I wanted to pretend to be annoyed, at that moment I couldn't.

"I'll see you soon", Andre said with a laugh.

"Okay. Bye."

I pressed 'End' on my phone, put it into my belt clip, rested my head against the wall and massaged my temples for a second. The quick moments of happiness that people who cared about me were giving out, were just that: moments. The whole ordeal was beginning to feel like an anchor around my neck.

I looked down to the end of the hallway. Denise was standing there, watching and waiting patiently. She probably hadn't moved an inch since she found me. I'd waited all my life for a woman that loved me, cared for me, and had my back the way she did, and there was no way to avoid dragging her into this foolishness, with the wrong results. Yet and still, it was hard for me to be anyone other than the man that I knew I was. At that very moment, I could have cried.

I broke the magnetic grip that the wall seemed to have on me, and slowly walked back to the end of the corridor.

"Is everything okay? Are you okay?" She asked as she looked up at me, like a mother concerned for her child.

I looked deeply into her eyes for a few seconds, and smiled while time stood still, and no one else was in the mall with us.

No, I'm not......

"I'll tell you about it over lunch. Let's go get us some gumbo, Gorgeous Lady..."

The Hot Seat

"Life is a series of natural and spontaneous changes. Don't resist them; that only creates sorrow. Let reality be reality. Let things flow naturally forward in whatever way they like."— Lao Tzu

December 18, 2010

Mr. William Powers
3767 S Mendenhall Rd
Memphis, TN 38115

RE: Interview

William:

Your interview to discuss your discipline

process has been scheduled for Tuesday, December 21, 2010.

Please report to your assigned installation at 9:00 am.

Regards,

Barbara
Officer-In-Charge

"Baby, this is overkill", I pleaded as Denise worked on the Full Windsor knot she was tying my tie into. "I don't want to wear a suit."

"Honey, Sweetie, Darling…" she rebutted, "The letter said "interview". So you should take it with the same seriousness that you would take being interviewed for a job. And in truth, you are interviewing for a job. It just so happens to be the job you already had", she said while trying not to smile too hard. "Besides…even murderers wear suits to court."

Did she just lump me in with murderers…?

"Baby", I said as I shot her a cynical look, "That's just a bunch of form letter jargon. No one is actually expecting me to look like an attorney from a downtown law firm. My peer group isn't exactly what you would call distinguished. I'm going to throw everyone around me into shock. On top of that, I watch plenty of court TV and the majority of defendants that I see look guilty."

She grabbed the tie right below the knot in mid-adjustment and pulled me down to her eye level with a quick snatch.

"Honey, Sweetie, Darling…you *are* guilty."

I stood there for a second with my mouth hanging open.

"Yeah, but…I'm…but that's…okay, I'm guilty, but with a very, very, VERY good exp-…………" I let out a heavy sigh. *Shit…*

Denise stood me up straight and began re-adjusting my tie. "Look Baby, I just don't want you to talk your way out of a job. Go in there in resolution mode, and try to put this behind you."

"I don't want to talk my way out of a job either, but I don't feel like I should have to mince words, for as long as I'm not being rude or condescending. You know me. The way it comes up is the way it comes out."

"Will…why do you have to be so bullheaded?" she asked.

"Oh, I don't know…probably for the same reason you have to be so official about everything…because it's the way you believe you should go about doing what you do." I laughed. "What I am, is honest…a character trait that seems to be an endangered species these days. But I bet you wouldn't be with me if I was any other way," I said with a smile.

"Well touché on that one, Mr. Guilty", she said as she flashed her smile right back at me, "But if I don't get you out of here soon you're going to be late. So let me grab your jacket…"

"Let's compromise…how about a sweater instead? I don't want to wear a jacket. That'll be more than dressy enough. Trust me."

"Okay, that's good enough", she conceded. "Now… what are you going to make absolutely certain that you do today?"

I shifted my eyes in both directions. "Make sure that no one has taken out an insurance policy on my life?" I asked with a raised eyebrow, while grinning like a Cheshire cat.

Before I even knew it, Denise had caught me with a quick jab to the solar plexus. As I sunk to her height from pain, I squealed with what little breath I had left, "Go into it with a resolution in mind."

"That's my guy", she said, and took the opportunity of us being at eye level and my lips being puckered to plant a kiss on me. *Okay, I had that one coming…but it still kinda hurt…*

We walked out to the living room together, and she shuffled past me and over to the coffee table and picked up something that looked like what she would take to work with her, opened it up, and held it out in front of me. I took it and opened it up.

"Okay, here's your planner", she said while presenting it like one of the Price Is Right girls, while it was in my hands. "You've got ink pens, a notepad, and all of your associated paperwork in here…"

"Oooooo, I even get to carry a "planner" today!" I said cynically, as I closed it and began waving it like a tambourine. "After I'm finished with my "interview", should I mosey on over to the university and loiter on the campus until someone grabs me by the arm and offers me a job?"

She made a motion to throw another body blow, which I quickly thwarted by blocking my mid-section with the planner. Then I reached out to grab her before she had time to react and pulled her close.

"I love you Denise! Words can never express just how much I love it when you don't hit me!" I rang out.

She laughed. I hugged her tightly and kissed her on her forehead. She looked up at me and smiled. Then we kissed passionately, as we would do when it was time to see each other off for the day. When we were done, she gently held my face in her hands.

"Resolution mode?" she asked softly.

"Resolution mode", I confirmed with a smile.

I tucked my planner under my arm and started strutting to the garage door. Denise gave me a butt-smack like a football player would give his teammate after making a drive-stopping play. I squeezed my butt cheeks together, stiffened up like a two-by-four, and let out a "Woo-hoo!" She cracked up. I grabbed the doorknob and just as I was about to walk out of the door she called out to me.

"Will…"

I turned around with raised eyebrows.

"Yes Love?" I asked attentively.

"Never stop standing on principle."

I smiled. She smiled back. I jumped into my car and backed out of the garage.

***

I rang the bell to the door leading into the office, to get into the building. Every time something of this nature took place, the combination code on the door locks was changed. So I had to wait to be let in. While waiting, I took a long, hard look at the man in the reflection of the door, and began wondering if a resolution was even possible…or worth it.

After about a minute, I see Tricia, the office secretary, power walking towards the door. She was another real sweetheart…with a temperament that I could only wish to have. I had never seen her get upset even once in my entire career, although more recently I had seen her frustrated quite a few times. That was a sure sign that the environment was toxic all around. She pushed the door open for me.

"Sharp dressed man!" she said with a big smile.

Guilty as sin... "Hey Trish."

"You're here for your interview, I take it?"

"That's right."

"Well everyone is kind of scattered right now, but I'll let Holly know you're here. Have a seat...here, use my chair. It's more comfortable." She looped her office chair around the desk and over to where I was standing.

"Are you sure? I don't want to put you out."

"I'm sure. I'm out on the floor right now anyway. I still have a way to go before I get to office work."

"Thanks."

She smiled. "No problem at all. I'll go get Holly. It's good to see you."

I smiled back. "It's good to see you, too."

The door leading out to the workroom floor was propped open. I positioned the chair in a way that would have me facing that doorway, sat down, and opened up my planner. I thought about Denise, laughed and shook my head. "Planner..."

Almost immediately, my co-workers began to

notice that I was in the building, and as usual, word travels fast on the workroom floor. All of a sudden, it seemed as if half of the office found a way to walk past the door and catch a glimpse of me, in my Sunday best. I got looks and waves and gestures that said everything from "Is that you?" to "Looking good!" to "I'm pulling for you!" to "See you back in here soon!" There were lots of smiles and 'thumbs-ups', all to which I respond-ed in kind. It was a good feeling to know that people cared when you thought they didn't even know what was going on. Ironically, without making it a point to intentionally look, I didn't see a single face in manage-ment.

After a couple of minutes, it seemed that just about everyone in the building had sent me their good vibrations, and I settled into the comfortable chair. I appreciated Tricia, if for no other reason than showing me just what kind of temperament was humanly pos-sible, no matter what was going on around you. It was beginning to feel like the only time and place in the world I could be alone with my thoughts was in that damn office...a place that I never had any business be-ing in to begin with.

I thought back to my initial interview, and just how much I had changed from the person I was back when I entered through that door for the very first time, to now. When I was hired, I was starry-eyed, Gung Ho, more than willing to work my way up to the healthy scenery I needed to see from day to day on the streets of our city (at least I accomplished that much), bubbling over with ideas to reinvent the service and take it right on into the next millennium. Hell only knew of the madness waiting for me just beyond those four walls. Management in this place was the absolute worst...the worst of the grassroots definition of 'managers', but even more so, the worst of human beings. I went from being willing to work off the clock in order to learn as much about the job as I could, to running out of any door that had an [EXIT] sign above it as quickly as possible...be it to get my work done or to go my merry way when the work day was finally over... and even then they wouldn't leave me alone. They wouldn't leave anybody alone. We couldn't simply let our work speak for us, they always wanted more. Like panhandlers on the street, no matter how much we gave them, it was never enough.

And then I got to thinking about my conversation with Nick the other night, and the form of purgatory that was our job...it was like being trapped in high school for the rest of your life. All of the favoritism, backstabbing, and teenager mentalities...the desks in the middle of the floor may as well have been a cuckoo's nest...a toll on the body and a tax on the brain of anyone in the building that had to do some tangible work while making any sort of attempt to live their lives above the fray, with a sense of normalcy. Some of the stuff taking place was so incredible I just *knew* that everyone would think I was making it up, dare I decided to speak on it outside of those four walls, with someone other than a co-worker. That's why my motto remained intact: don't take work home, and don't take home to work. It was almost as if the supervisors were all standing around viewing me from a distance, saying to themselves, "Wow...here's a guy that's hard-working, dedicated, happy with himself and where he is in life, and doesn't seem fazed by this place......we'll fix that!"

I didn't realize just how long I had been sitting there with my thoughts, until I saw Holly headed towards me. As I broke out of my spell and sat up straight, I noticed she was shuffling to put on her coat and hold on to her paperwork, while simultaneously walking towards the door, and she had a cigarette dangling from her mouth.

I greeted her just as she hit the doorway. "Hey Holly. Smoke break?"

"Kinda", she replied. "Your interview is in the big house. I figured I'd light up on the way there."

The "big house" was how we commonly referred to the bulk warehouse, a building about five times the size of ours, on the opposite end of the gigantic parking lot. That injected a bit of nervousness into me.

"Oh really? Why is it there?" I asked as we headed out of the door.

"They actually have a couple of court team members available this morning. You'll be interviewing with them. Barbara's downtown conducting business with district, so I know she won't be there, but Emma and Liz might be...and their objective will be to try and rile you up, to prove to the higher powers that you're a savage. So I need you to be on your best behavior. You look nice, by the way."

"Thank you." *And thank you too, Andre...*

"You're welcome. So, yeah...be polite, be courteous, answer all questions as thoroughly as you can, and keep your cool...even if it kills you."

"I got it. That sounds easy enough..." *...so long as there's no acting involved. Can I kill them instead? That's probably not acceptable...*

"Good. Slow your pace down a bit. You're outrunning my cigarette."

"Sorry about that. I haven't lost my pace...yet."

Holly laughed as she blew out a puff of smoke that the winter air blew right back into her eyes. It caught her off guard.

"You won't have time to lose it. You'll be back in the saddle in no time", she said while trying to shake off the mist. As she let out a couple of coughs, I put my planner under my arm, put my hands into my pockets, and slowed down the pace.

As we approached the front doors of the building, Holly stopped short about a dozen steps to get a couple more puffs in, before tossing the half-smoked cigarette into the grass. I waited at the door until she was done, then when she started moving again I held the door open for her.

We jumped on the elevator and Holly pushed (3). On the ride up, she asked me, "How do you feel?"

"I feel pretty good!" I replied. "I'm ready and waiting to clear my name."

"Well that's what I wanna hear", she said. "Let's get this over with."

"Music to my ears", I said.

We stepped off of the elevator and began a walk down the long hallway. I'd never been in this building before, so I couldn't help taking a peek into all the doorways we passed.

"I never knew there was so much office space", I said, partially bewildered.

"Yep, loads of it…on every floor…mostly occupied by people with cushy middle management positions."

"I'm beginning to think I chose the wrong craft."

She laughed. "Nah, you're great at what you do. Well respected by all that know you."

"On the street, that is. Be sure to specify that. I'm well hated in the office."

"Oh quit it. No one hates you. Your co-workers have loads of respect for you. They think you're one of the smartest and brightest people to ever do this, even if they never admit it publicly."

"Really?" I asked.

"Really", she stated bluntly. "And believe it or not Will", she said, "Despite this occurrence, management respects you too."

"Well it must be for something other than standing up for myself, because all this time I've done my damnedest to not get into it wit-"

"Here, here we are…308", Holly interrupted, as we had reached our destination.

Holly grabbed the handle and pushed the door open. Inside was a conference room that looked like it belonged somewhere inside the Pentagon, where war strategies were born. Everyone inside was upbeat and conversing among themselves from both sides of the table, with their coffee mugs in front of them, like the cast of a morning news program during segues. Holly walked in and began greeting everyone, and I followed not-too-closely, while keeping quiet and forcing myself to wear a smile, sort of the way you feel when walking into a room full of family that isn't your own. There was a woman that I didn't know, but would've guessed by the way she was dressed that she was – yep, you guessed it – an attorney from a downtown law firm, sitting in the first chair on the right. It was the first thing I noticed about anyone there...consciously, of course. In a weird way, it made me feel a little at ease because now I didn't feel like I was the only one dressed for a courtroom...even if I was on trial. Andre was sitting next to her, bragging about a double-double he had in a game last week, being his usual cocky self, and the women were signifying each other about Andre being his usual cocky self.

There was an empty chair sitting at the end of the table. I looked down at it, and the smile left my face. I stood behind it with both hands in front of me, gripping my planner tightly, and waiting for the proper protocol.

Holly went around the end of the table and sat down next to Andre. Liz was sitting directly across from the woman I didn't know, holding down her side of the table, holding up her end of the conversation, and trying her best to not look at me. Emma wasn't there. *...coward...* It was funny how everyone seemed to have been working there for decades on end and knew everyone else, via one avenue or another. At first observation, it certainly didn't seem like a place or an atmosphere where I'd get my head chopped off for simply telling my version of the truth.

During a break in the last bit of laughter, the woman that I didn't know stood up and put her hand on the back of the chair at the end of the table, and looked at me. "This one here's for the guest of honor."

That brought my smile back, as I looked up. "Yeah, right!" I said as I laughed out loud and the chatter in the room went on without the two of us.

She laughed as she took a couple of steps toward me and extended a handshake. "Hello Will. I'm Jennifer."

"Oh, you know me?" I asked as I shook her hand. "Oh…I guess you kinda do, huh? Duh…"

Her laugh was a bit heightened. "Yeah, I kinda do. I have your file in front of me. Not the way I prefer to meet people, but these things happen and we have to get to the bottom of them", she said with a big smile and her head tilted sideways.

"A member of the court team, I presume?" I asked.

"Yes…Andre and myself", she replied as she extended her arm in his direction. She was a very attractive woman. Bubbly, and seemingly sweet…not at all what I was expecting to see or encounter. I wanted to turn on the charm, but I was feeling like that soon-to-be euthanized Basset Hound all over again, so I just maintained my manners and poise. Plus, Denise's words were resonating inside my head: *…you should take it with the same seriousness that you would take being interviewed for a job…* Then I thought about her being in the same room with me turning on the charm for another woman, and my stomach reminded me that she didn't hit like a girl. So no, charm was not appropriate in this instance.

Jennifer gestured for me to have a seat, and I did, while sitting the planner down on the table in front of me. The talking and the laughter died down shortly thereafter.

"Okay, I think we can get down to business now", Jennifer stated as everyone began settling in and shuffling their paperwork in front of them. I settled in as well, but it really felt more like I was sinking. My butterflies felt more like bumblebees, and they began doing their exotic dance inside my gut.

"Will...I've already read your statement on the events of the day in question, and I've read management's statement as well. What we'd really, really like to do is have this resolved between the parties involved, and keep this matter from even reaching our level. I only have a few questions that I'd like to ask you, and I want you to feel free to elaborate as you wish. Is that okay with you?"

It appeared as if I had the undivided attention of everyone except Liz, who still didn't seem too interested in making eye contact with me.

"That's perfect", I said as I lifted my head. *..."The truth is your best defense"...*

"Great", she said. "Okay, question number one... what's your quality of life like? Have you been dealing with any circumstances with your health, or away from the job, that might cause your demeanor to be a little off-kilter before you start your work day?"

Andre and Holly looked up from their papers and over at me.

I paused. *...I guess this is your opening, huh?*

"Well", I said as I leaned forward, "I don't know if this helps or hurts my case, but the truth is that my quality of life is immaculate. I have a clean bill of health, I'm in pretty good physical shape for my age...or at least I'd like to think that I am. I've avoided just about every pitfall that life has thrown at anyone that has said hello and goodbye to 40 years of age, my immediate family circle has not been broken by death, diseases or accidents, I'm married to an absolutely wonderful woman that has my back in every way imaginable, and we just moved into a new home that will be our team project in the weeks and months to come. My bills are paid, my investments are on track, and my retirement plan is coming along just fine. I've never in my life used an illegal drug, I don't abuse alcohol...well, not before this incident I didn't, but I believe I've earned my one lapse in judgment over the weekend..." That brought laughs from everyone.

"...and my biggest complaint in life before the

morning of this incident was how the Titans would still have a shot at home field advantage in the wild card round if they played in the NFC West. So, no…nothing else to look towards for a source of frustration. It begins and ends with the environment that management in my station fosters on the workroom floor."

Andre gave me a look of extreme confusion. Holly made a throat-slashing motion with her hand. I looked at her the way that Andre was looking at me.

"Okay", said Jennifer, with a look of surprise as she searched for a piece of paper other than the one she had on top. "That leads me directly to question number two; is your perception of management really that low?"

"Well I can't speak for any other station", I said with a shrug as Jennifer nodded, "but number one…in our station, micromanagement has run amuck. They feel the need to have their fingerprint on every single thing in the office, and they act as if they have all the sense and their workers have none…when in fact the truth is actually much closer to the opposite. This instance is a perfect example…which leads ME directly to number two…" I laughed at myself as I clasped my hands together.

"Number two…normally, if someone's feeling overburdened by their workload, management usually contacts other workers, then those workers contact the overburdened individual and they meet up on the street in order to divvy up the work. Not once before this incident had management ever come out to me on the street to take work off of me. There had been a few instances where they brought work *to* me…but take work *from* me? Never. What would be the point? It's not like they were going to immediately take it to someone else and tell them to stop what they were doing at the moment and go do the work that they had taken from me, and they definitely weren't going to do the work themselves…which brings up another interesting point about that day…who's manning the asylum while all of this is going on? This was so urgent and so important that it took *two* of them coming out to me? I asked that question to the head manager in charge after I was forced back to the station that day, and I got some mumbo-jumbo about one being a witness for the other. A witness to *what* exactly?"

"It's interesting that you brought that up", Jennifer said. "I was reading their statement and I thought it interesting that – what's your supervisor's name?"

"Emma", I answered. My mentioning Emma's name snapped Liz out of her trance for long enough to catch the remaining words in Jennifer's sentence.

"Right, Emma", she continued "I thought it interesting that she felt that she would need someone to go with her to corroborate her story. That leads me to believe that a story was what they went out to get for themselves, rather than part of your daily assignment from you."

Liz didn't miss a beat at that point. "Well…" she said right before clearing her throat. The second I heard her voice, I then became the one no longer interested in making eye contact. I stared straight ahead, and tried to keep my eyes from squinting and jaw line from shrinking. Red spots started to emerge in the atmosphere.

"Emma was sort of …concerned for her own safety, as she felt that Will was um…" Liz cleared her throat once again, "….acting erratic that morning…"

I interjected, "But not so erratic that she couldn't keep herself from immediately following me out to my route…"

I could see without looking directly at her that cutting Liz off the way I did sent another jolt through her spine, as she seemed to have a knee-jerk reaction to my mere presence. Holly raised her left hand up off of the table to give me a sly little 'take it easy' signal. I let out a sigh, and refocused squarely on Jennifer, as the redness subsided. "That just doesn't sound like something that someone who was concerned for her safety would do", I said while giving my best lawyer impersonation. Jennifer nodded in agreement to my offering.

"I mean", I pleaded, "If I was in charge, and I can

see that someone is clearly agitated...even if I felt that I was clearly in the right, if I saw that they stormed off in what I felt was a huff, then I'd like to think that I would refocus on more pressing issues at that moment and give them a period of time to cool off before trying to re-engage them or resurrect the issue...especially if the issue wasn't pressing. That, in my eyes, is how effective management operates. And this issue was hardly pressing. Absolutely nothing could be done with what they came out to get from me for at least another five hours. They were looking for a confrontation." *They got one...*

Andre and Holly watched and listened intently. Liz rubbed her nose and went on with daydreaming about whatever had her mind captivated.

"Well I'd like to thank you for being the perfect lead into my questions", Jennifer said with a short glance at her paperwork. "This last one isn't so much a question as it is a statement, but I certainly would like for you to convey your thoughts...yes, a confrontation ensued, and you made a statement to your supervisor on the street that day that you were going to – and I paraphrase here – "mule kick her right in her teeth". That's a pretty graphic picture, Will...not to mention a specific intent."

Eh, boy... I looked over my right shoulder as if to find my good conscience hovering.

You could have heard a feather hit the table. It was almost as if the world had stopped spinning. Andre and Holly refocused on their papers in front of them. Liz was now looking for something on the ceiling. Jennifer's voice lowered to an innocently soft tone.

"You wanna tell me what was going through your mind when you said that?"

"Obviously nothing good..." I said jokingly, "...but I had been forced into the role of villain. I knew for a fact that I was being fed a bunch of lies back at the station, I *left* the station for the sole intent of not keeping an argument going, and regardless of what's said to the contrary by any of the parties involved, they didn't catch up to me to try to provide some sort of relief. While I was still in the station, I was told that it wasn't going to take as long as I said it would take to finish all of that work that I was given. So why did they all of a sudden flip like a flapjack and run out to the street to get work from me? I hadn't been working for a full 15 minutes before this one here and her crony came barreling down on me", I said while wagging my finger in the direction of Liz. "It was all about Emma getting the last word, which she had been denied. That's the whole thing in a nutshell. So then, even after I saw them and they continued on with the confrontation, I still just wanted to go on with my day. I was trying to refrain from engaging them because I knew that I had nothing good to say to them at that time. No soap. Their M.O. was "stop what you're doing right now and do ONLY what we tell you to do", like drill sergeants. And THEN...I was threatened with the police. That's right, Emma was ready, willing and able to drag the police into this and waste law enforcement's time and taxpayer dollars because a man simply wanted to do his job. So with that threat imminent, they THEN felt like they had me in the palm of their hands. So while they're giving me a direct order, they were simultaneously preventing me from carrying that order out...you know, to get their last digs in. So, allow me to recap: I was dumped on, then lied to, then goaded into an argument that I chose to ignore, then followed, then *forced* into a confrontation, then threatened with being arrested, then harassed."

I paused. Jennifer was intensely focused on me and absorbing every syllable coming out of my mouth. She had turned in her chair and was facing me directly. With her hands folded together, she was gripping the knee on her crossed leg. The one foot that was touching the floor was silently tapping the carpet. Liz was still looking anywhere other than at me...now sort of staring into space in between Jennifer and Andre's heads. She seemed to be frozen somewhere within her own guilt the whole time. Andre was subtly giving me an affirmative nod, with a 'that's my boy' expression. Holly had facepalmed herself.

...... *"The truth is your best defense"......* *

"...I was angry. And I don't know any human being alive who wouldn't have been angry in that same situation."

There was a brief moment of silence, which was broken by Jennifer. "Okay, well I think we have a much clearer view of what went on now, and that said, hopefully we can wrap this up rather quickly, get you back to your route as soon as possible, and we can all move on with our lives," she gave a quick glance to the others in the room, "Okay, unless anyone has anything else...?"

Liz shook her head neurotically. Andre shook his head convincingly. Holly shook her head while rubbing her temples.

"Okay, well it looks like that's it!" Jennifer said as she began to rise up out of her chair. Will...thank you so much for coming, and thanks for your cooperation."

I rose to my feet and extended an official handshake, with a smile. "Thank you for having me, thank you for your questions, and thank you for listening." I waved to the group. "Thanks to all of you."

Holly's pace down the hallway was crisp and much

faster than normal. I was easily a foot taller than her, and I was struggling to keep up. At my normal pace, people usually struggled to keep up with me. We got on the elevator, and she reached into her shirt pocket for her cigarettes. I knew she was upset with my way of handling the interview, but at that point, I really didn't care anymore about how she or anyone else felt. I felt liberated, and was genuinely proud of my offering. She waited until we hit the front doors of the building before breaking the silence.

"What did you do that for?" She asked in an aggravated tone.

"What did I do *what* for?" I asked in an aggravated tone.

"Make it sound like this place is the one and only source of your problems. *That* 'what'", she snapped while patting all of her pockets in search for her lighter.

And once again, just as it was on that fateful day, I'd had it. The tipping point was finally reached, and I was sick and tired of playing nice. I wasn't going to stand for my methods and my character being brought into question by anyone for another second. I raised my eyes and my hands to the heavens, and let my outside voice rip.

"Because that's the TRUTH!! Why is everyone in this place so deathly afraid of the simple TRUTH?! Why does everyone try to act as if this place doesn't have the power to change someone's demeanor? This place would turn Gandhi into a cynical asshole! And people in this place have been lying to themselves about just what the truth really is for so long, that they can't even distinguish between fantasy and reality anymore! The woman asked questions, and I answered them. Honestly!" I looked directly at her while in mid-stride. "Just whose side are you on, anyway?"

"Don't try to make this about me, or the way that I have to approach these cases", Holly said. "My job standing isn't in question. No one's shining a light in my face. They're shining it in *your* face. And when they're shining a light in your face, they're looking for something specific, and you didn't even come close to providing it. I'm trying to help you, and you're not helping me to help you."

"You're trying to help me by expecting me to paint a phony picture that refuses to touch on what's really happening here?" I asked. "Well you sure do have a funny way of showing that you're trying to help me, and maybe that's why I can't help you to help me. And in that case, maybe I don't need your help, because help isn't what it really is. "

"Well I sure as hell hope you know what you're doing", she said, "because in case you didn't know… the powers that be around here don't like to feel as if they're being blamed for much of anything, let alone creating hostile work environments."

"Well that's too damn bad, because that's exactly what they do, and I'm tired of tiptoeing around that simple fact. Damn near everything that the "powers that be" have their fingers on leads me to conclude that they actually exist in some parallel universe where no one ever comes within one hundred feet of manual labor. So to hell with them. I'm part of the group down here in the trenches dealing with this shit on a daily basis. If the "powers that be" care that little about the very people that help them achieve their oh-so-heralded numbers, then this is no longer the place for me anyway. Whoever wants this crap is more than welcome to it."

I had gotten on such a good roll, that I didn't realize that I had already walked right past my car. I looked over my shoulder, did a double take, and stopped mid-shuffle. *...what am I headed back into that hellhole for...*

Holly rolled her eyes, stopped her pace, and made a half-circle so she could face my new direction. "Okay, fine. You gotta be Sinatra and do it your way? FINE. But I need to inform you that you just painted yourself into a corner back there by going into explicit detail and admitting to your state of mind that day, all while badmouthing your superiors and admitting to being insubordinate. You may feel good about yourself, but I just hope that you didn't talk your way right out of your damn job."

I stopped and did my own one-eighty, and started shouting from our distance.

"So what if I did? There was life before this place, there'll be life after it", I said matter-of-factly. "And if that's what it comes down to, then they'll both be of a much higher quality than life DURING this place. That's the whole damn problem right there. These jack-asses don't want you to work for them. They want you to LIVE for them! Screw that. Money doesn't rule my world. I need my life back...before I have every ounce of life sucked out of me, for sucking every ounce of life out of somebody else. And as I recall, there wasn't a single need of mine that wasn't being met with less money rolling in. So there...I just had my epiphany. Don't worry about going to bat for me. Not for anoth-er second. Let my words stand on their own merit. If they aren't good enough for the "powers that be", then every last one of you can have your red wagon back. It was never meant for me anyway."

Holly tilted her head to the side and asked with the most confused of looks, "What the hell are you talking about?"

"You heard me. Figure it out", I blurted as I turned away from her and started walking again.

"FINE!" Holly retorted.

"You're damn right it's fine!"

I could feel her watching me as I walked away. She was waiting for me to say 'thanks' or 'goodbye' or something. I didn't have anything for her. I made a bee-line to my car like I was about to beat it up, unlocked it with the remote, got inside, and shut the door unceremoniously. I cut my eyes in the direction of where she was when she stopped walking. She was standing a few feet away from the huge gate leading out of the parking lot, in the path of would-be traffic, using the folder that contained her case paperwork to shield the flame on her lighter from the wind, as she held it up to the cigarette dangling from her lips. The woman smoked more than Popeye.

I stuck my key into the ignition, started up the car, backed out of the parking space, and zipped off of the parking lot.

The Verdict

"Sooner or later, everyone sits down to a banquet of consequences."— *Robert Louis Stevenson*

December 23, 2010

Mr. William Powers
3767 S Mendenhall Rd
Memphis, TN 38115

RE: Conflict Resolution Team Case #14796145

William:

This letter confirms our post-disciplinary interview for emergency procedure on December 20, 2010.

FORWARD TIME EXPIRED

It was determined by a team vote of 6 for and 3 against, that your employment is terminated with cause, effective immediately.

Your employment has been terminated because of your conduct while on duty on the afternoon of Thursday, December 16, 2010. The act of threatening a superior with physical violence is a gross violation of our Company Code of Conduct and Zero Tolerance Policy.

Payment of your accrued annual leave will be included in your final paycheck, which will be mailed to you. You can expect a separate letter that will outline the status of your retirement savings and health benefits, and your options going forward. We have already received your identification badge, and it is also required that you return all of your uniform apparel to your installation within seven (7) days of receipt of this letter.

You will need to keep the company informed of your contact information so that we are able to provide information you may need in the future, such as your W-2 form.

GODFREY WILSON III

We regret that this action is necessary. Please call if you should need any assistance with your transition. We wish you the best in all of your future endeavors.

Regards,

Barbara
Officer-In-Charge
The Court Team – REF:

The Aftermath

"Do not take life too seriously. You will never get out of it alive."— Elbert Hubbard

It was a day above ground, which means it was a good day...so far. Old Man Winter had finally bid his farewell, and the spring flowering on the myrtle and dogwood trees in our backyard had already began to bud and gaze over the merging highways, along with the birds that seemed to love perching themselves there. I had just finished preparing a decent lunch... one that I'd get to sit down to in adequate comfort, and eat like a human being, in a reasonable amount of time. I turned around to abide by our 'first one into the kitchen' rule and make a pot of coffee, when Denise came through the doorway, rubbing her eyes like a toddler.

"Good morning Gorgeous."

"Good morning Handsome. You're so sweet...handling the coffee duties", she said.

"Hey, I want some too", I replied. "I know better than to think that I have any servants around here. Besides, I'm not that far removed from bachelorhood. I haven't forgotten how to do *everything* for myself... yet", I said with a grin.

"Whatever." She leaned against the island while waiting for her body to realize that it was awake, and peered over into my lunch pail.

"You know, Love...you don't have to make sandwiches for lunch every day anymore. You actually get to sit down in a break room, or at your desk, and take your time to eat and help your food digest...as your mother says. And you also have access to a refrigerator and a microwave now."

"I know, you're right", I said as I affirmed her statement with a nod. "But I'm actually pretty fond of sandwiches. Quick and easy, no containers needed, and no mess to clean up afterwards. Besides, didn't you say that microwaves were of the devil?" I asked sarcastically.

"If you don't cut it out, you're going to get to ask him personally." She said with a snarl and curled lip.

"Well alrighty then! You're awake after all!" I exclaimed. "Let me get to gettin'..."

I pushed the [ON/OFF] button on the coffee

maker, and then turned back to the island to finish putting everything inside my lunch pail.

And then I paused. I looked over at Denise, and she asked, "What's the matter?" That was her favorite question to ask, even though 95% of the time, absolutely nothing was the matter. But this instance was a part of that remaining 5%…and a serious matter for me.

"Sorry Love", I said, "I'm just having a moment of guilt. I remember you warning me to not be so bull-headed, and I didn't heed that warning. And now, as a result, we're dealing with less money coming through the door. I apologize to you for taking us backwards with my stubbornness. Please forgive me."

"Oh, baby…" she said as she came and put her arms around my waist, "That little financial hit we've taken is like getting pelted with a marshmallow. You had your education and prior work experience to fall back on, I'm due for a promotion at the end of this semester, and you've been talking about putting some legs behind your idea for a home-based basketball clothing and apparel business. We're doing just fine. You did what you felt like you had to do, and in turn, your old company did you a favor."

I put my arm around her.

"Well I'm really glad to hear that you feel that way", I said. "I do in fact feel like a mountain of pressure and stress has been lifted off of my mind and back now that I'm out of there...I think I just needed to hear you say that you're not upset about it."

"Will, you're a great man that takes care of me and your entire family to the best of your ability", she professed. "I have the utmost confidence in you, no matter what road you choose now, and in the future. I'll support you the way you support me."

"What about when it's time to mow the lawn?" I asked as I looked down at her.

"I'll bring you lemonade", she said while pretending to strain her neck to look up at me.

I laughed. "It's a deal. Okay, gotta see what this day has in store for me. I'd love for you to stay joined to my hip...not!"

"I don't like you either!" she said as she took her arms from around my waist and pushed herself away from my body. I laughed and turned to the cabinet to where we kept the coffee mugs and disposable cups with lids. I reached inside and grabbed her favorite mug.

"You know..." I said as I poured her java first, "... progress is predicated on your finances increasing, not decreasing."

"We'll always make progress", she said while accepting her mug with both hands, "Because you're a man with a plan!"

"And you're a woman with a plan! That's why we fit together."

"This is true." We smiled at each other.

I finished my pour, snapped the lid onto my travel cup and moved it over to the island, closed up my lunch pail and zipped it, then went to give Denise an already-anticipated peck on her coffee-covered lips. I matched her pucker and gave her a peck.

"Ooh baby, the dragon…it's coming through your nostrils. Slay that, slay that."

"Shut up", she said, making the face that I loved to provoke.

I cracked up laughing, slung my lunch pail over my shoulder and grabbed my morning cup of joe. Just as I hit the kitchen doorway, Denise called me.

"Will…"

I stopped and raised my eyebrows for her.

"Never stop standing on principle."

I couldn't contain my smile. *She knows.*

"Love you."

"Love you too."

***

I was sitting at my desk, trying my absolute hardest to fall in love with the ball and chain all over again, and show my appreciation for all of the strings that Denise pulled with her colleagues in order to get me a technical writing gig…but failing miserably. Even after a month of being back in the marketing field, I still found myself daydreaming quite often. The time was split evenly, drifting away with thoughts of being my own boss and wondering who my customers were now in the hands of. I wondered if they ever even thought of me. The gig I now held really wasn't all that bad, and neither was the company...I just had determined long ago that white collar America and tiny little cubicles simply weren't for me, and here I was, right back in the same position I was in all those years ago, when I decided that it was time to go after what I really wanted.

"9:30...break time!" someone in the vicinity shouted. My department was on the second floor, and seemed to be riddled with smokers, which was the reason for the mating call. Smokers don't miss their chances to light up for anything. We all hit the stairwell, but I always made it a point to stay several paces behind the take-our-break-outside group. In addition to the nicotine that seemed as if it was coming out of their pores, they never seemed to talk about much outside of the three things I made it a point to never talk about at the job: race, religion and politics.

We all hit the side door of the building, and I moved upwind of the smokers. And at 9:32, right on cue with me stepping into the sunlight, my phone began to buzz on my hip. I reached for it and pressed 'Answer'...

"What's up Chris?" I asked as I leaned against the wall.

"Will my man…how are you making it?"

"Still haven't figured that part out yet. I guess I need another month or so", I said while trying to feign enthusiasm. "But hey…it's good to have a job, right?"

"You got that right. Especially so soon after…how's the Mrs.?" He asked, changing the course in mid-flight so as not to state the obvious. We had kept in contact with each other almost weekly since Christmas, but every time we talked or saw each other at league games, my removal was the five thousand pound elephant in the room or on the telephone line.

"The Mrs. is fine…still trying to get me interested in purchasing a motorcycle, so we can see the country together. It won't happen in this lifetime…at least not that way it won't."

"Just take the bitch seat on hers", Chris joked. "She'll take care of you."

"Uh, no, she won't", I quickly replied. "You'll be the bitch before me."

"Ha ha ha", he said dryly. "Well…you want the good news first or the bad news first?"

"Bad news."

"Always the bad news first", Chris said with a humorous edge. Then he let out a sigh, and paused for a couple of seconds. "The appeal was denied, and the arbitrator finalized the decision yesterday afternoon."

"Humph."

"The good news is", he said before letting me get too entrenched in my thoughts, "We did win back pay for you. So you'll be getting that in a lump sum. The somewhere-in-between news is…a decision still hasn't been made on your pension. So you might still get that in full, as well as your sick leave. You are, however, going to have to opt out of the 401(k) plan though. They say it's strictly employees only."

"Hey Chris", I replied, "Anything that I get beyond what I had in my hands when I walked out of that door in uniform for the last time, is thanks to you. So I appreciate the victories and the defeats, because it means that someone gave enough of a damn to fight."

"Hey man, it's been an honor. It couldn't have happened to a better man. Can't just sit around and not do anything. I just wish I could do more…or to be specific, right the one wrong that we all want righted and get you back in here, where you belong."

"Hey, I wish there was something I could do to change that outcome myself. The funny part about that is, I'm still not so sure that I would've handled my end of things any differently. But hey, the cards have been dealt."

"And the wheels of justice turn ever so slowly", he added. "Your people on 4 are *pissed*. A whole lot of them are starting to get the real story, bit by bit."

I perked up. "Really? They're asking about me?"

"All the time", Chris said. "God only knows what they're being told when they call the station, but one thing can't be denied…their respect for you as a worker and as a man can't be swayed. They knew what they had in you…and they're starting to figure out that what they hear on the other end of a phone conversation doesn't hold water. So they're starting to grab a hold of whoever they see in the neighborhood at any given time and get the real scoop. They miss you. We miss you too."

"And I miss you all's crazy asses", I said with a smile. "I built up some pretty strong bonds with a lot of my former customers. Now that I know for certain that I won't be seeing them any more in a professional capacity… I had probably better make a few phone calls. Maybe make some sort of arrangement to get as many of them together as possible, to tell my side of the story and let them know I'm okay… and apologize."

"I'm sure they'd appreciate that", Chris said with confidence.

I looked over and noticed that the nicotine crowd had begun filing back into the building. Break time had elapsed.

"Well, looks like I have to end this now."

"Yeah, I gotta get some work done myself", he

said as I could hear a stern voice echo "Break time's over!" in the background.

"Tell everyone in the trenches I said hello, and give them my regards."

"For sure. Oh, and one last thing real quick… Craig wanted me to tell you to call him. He quit."

"Did he??"

"Yep. Waited until the day after President's Day and called Emma's no-good lying ass five minutes before time for all of us to clock in, to tell her to shove her bullshit up her tailpipe. Workload was hell that day, but the overtime was my spending money for the month!"

We both laughed.

"Good for him!" I said. "Got y'all good, huh?"

"Well, actually he didn't. He had slyly let all of us know that he was taking a job back in Birmingham, prior to that moment. He even had let on to some of the customers on different routes that knew him by name. So shortly after clocking on that morning, they rounded all of us up in the middle of the floor to start their hate campaign. As soon as 'One of your co-workers has quit on you' passed through Emma's lips, we all let out a cheer. They're so stupid, they thought we were cheering because we hated the guy."

We both laughed again. I felt like I had just watched the son I never had walk across the stage at commencement to receive his MBA.

"He said his number hasn't changed", Chris said.

"Duly noted. That's one call I won't procrastinate with making."

"And of course, we'll cross paths in league."

"Of course! I still owe you a triple double from the start of the season, and my team owes yours one good shellacking. And I won't be late for any more games now either."

"It won't make any difference when you play us." He said with the smugness of a three-peat NBA champion.

"I'm going to personally make you eat those words."

He laughed. "Whatever. Alright brother, catch you later."

"Later."

I pressed 'End' on my phone, and put it into my belt clip. All had gone back inside except for me. I closed my eyes, rested my head against the wall, and let out a huge sigh.

And then, in the anxiety of that moment…I made an arbitrary decision to take the rest of the day off. I walked around the side of the building to the front parking lot while pulling my keys out of my pocket. I detected my car, got into it, and left the rest of my work day where it was sitting.

I took the not-so-scenic route on this day…didn't want to give myself too much time to second-guess my decision. I wanted to say something, write something, leave something somewhere, let everyone know that I loved them and would never hurt them meaningfully…but I figured that if fate had it in the cards, I'd get my chance someday. I had to lend myself to the cause. Nah, my family, friends, teammates and co-workers wouldn't understand…they'd just try to talk me out of it…tell me how much I was needed here on earth. But I knew they'd all get along just fine without me…they were strong. And there were some vile, disgusting people that the planet needed to rid itself of. I couldn't leave this one up to God…the probabilities of Him being too busy to handle it in due time were too high. Sure, my thoughts were cruel and heartless, but they were turned that way by actions that were cruel and heartless. These serpents thought that playing with people's livelihood was all a big joke. They needed to be stopped…before they could do the same thing to someone else. As I headed east on I-240 and approached the 385 exit, I looked to my left and subtly waved 'goodbye' to my privacy wall.

I drove around to the back of the station and parked on the opposite side of the brick support wall, where it would be extremely easy for my vehicle to blend in with those of the window customers. I got out of my car, popped the trunk, and grabbed my backpack – that was loaded with essentials – by one of its straps, reserved for this very day. An air of vengeance loomed ominous...

I walked past the line of window customers and right into the building. It's too easy when they're not expecting you. I slipped my backpack off of my shoulders, reached into it and grabbed my tools, making sure I had the correct grip in each hand, and let the backpack fall to the floor, as I bent my elbows and raised the barrel of each tool to the ceiling. The room turned scarlet red.

I looked to my right...Emma had her back to me, Liz was facing me, and they both were doing the usual...something totally irrelevant to the main objective. That was perfect and played right into my grand appearance. I began walking towards them. Someone in the customer line that I had just walked past yelled out "GUN!!"...thus ruining my timing. I wanted to get a little closer to them before someone noticed, but I had to be ready.

Liz looked up and saw me. Her eyes expanded to the size of saucers, and fear completely paralyzed her. Emma still had yet to realize that her number had been pulled, as she was still looking at some report on her computer screen with her hand on the mouse.

Idiot... * She possessed the voice that I could stand the least, so before she could even realize what was upon her and let some superficial plea for her life escape from her lips, I used my right trigger finger to put two slugs in her back.

I had everyone's undivided attention from that moment. As heads popped out of workspaces and Emma's lifeless body slowly slumped over the desk, I once again raised the barrels of my tools to the ceiling, spun around in a circle in the middle of the floor, and made a public service announcement...

"IF I SEE A CELL PHONE, YOU DIE!!"

Screams and pandemonium ensued. Everybody covered their heads, ducked down as low as they could, and began stampeding for the exits. I quickly looked over at the boss's office, just in time to see Barbara in the doorway, looking around to try and figure out what was happening. I raised my left hand to aim at her. The heads of a couple of co-workers zoomed through my focal plane. I blinked repeatedly. She saw me, and almost jumped straight up into the air as she retreated back into the office and slammed the door shut.

Liz used my minor distraction to break away from the grip of fear, and tried to make a break for the door. Her physical condition made her final decision on Earth a bad one. I used my left hand to aim for her leg. The first shot missed and ricocheted off of a metal support beam and almost took out a co-worker before settling into the wall plaster. That would've been bad. So I thought I had better concentrate a little harder on my target. I kept my aim steady as I squinted and put a slug in her left thigh while in mid-stride. The sting of hot lead tearing through flesh caused her to fall to the ground and shriek in pain. I heard glass breaking over in a far corner of the building, immediately followed by the fire alarm. Someone had tripped it, in the hopes of an adjacent building coming to their aid. I let off a shot in the direction of the ringing bell. More screaming and scrambling for freedom continued as the building was rapidly being abandoned recklessly. I slowly walked over to Liz, who now was unsuccessfully trying to drag herself across the floor to salvation while smearing a trail of blood across the floor. I used my right foot to push her over onto her back, as she grimaced. As I stood over her and looked into her fear-packed eyes, she reached down to the bullet's point of entry, and began shaking uncontrollably.

"Didn't think I had it in me, did you?"

She screamed out with every ounce of life that remained in her body.

"Shut up bitch", I said, and gave her one more slug between the eyes.

Out of my peripheral vision, I caught someone running towards me, and I turned to see who it was…

Chris. I pointed my right hand at him and stopped him dead in his tracks, as his hands raced for the ceiling.

"This is not the hour of the hero. Get out of this building."

"So you're gonna kill *me* now?" Chris asked through his pain.

"Not if you don't make me", I stated with a cold heart. "You don't deserve it. They do. You're not who I came here for, so don't make me waste a perfectly good life and a perfectly good bullet…"

I looked to my left and could see Barbara through the doorway leading to the secretary's office. Her office had another door that led into that office. She had run out of her office and into the adjacent one, and was frantically trying to get out of the building through the door that I had already disabled from the outside. She thought about trying to make another run for it through the second office door. While keeping my right hand pointed at Chris, I used my left hand to aim at the office doorway and let off a round that ripped through the drywall to the left of the doorway. She let out a wild scream, used the door frame to abruptly stop herself from running out of the office, and then slammed the door to that office shut. I redirected my left hand to accompany my right.

"I have business to tend to. Get moving. Now."

"Will, man please…just listen-"

"I'm telling you for the last time. Get OUT of this building."

He hesitated for a couple of seconds, as the glum realization that love wasn't going to conquer this battle fell down upon him.

"Live the rest of your life as if I never existed", I said with an affirmative nod.

As his eyes welled, he dropped his hands, turned, and ran for the back door.

I strolled over to the boss's office, and gave the lock on the door two good pops. I heard Barbara scream wildly again as she was trying with all her might to push the office desk over to the door and barricade herself in, but she couldn't contain herself for long enough to muster up the strength, or was simply too weak to move it quickly enough. I kicked the door open and she let out a squeal, as she stood there with her hands in fists, trembling like a tree limb in a hurricane.

"Andre's boy, huh? Should have been fired a long time ago, huh? Do I have it right?"

"The police are on their way!" She said through her hysteria.

"What good is that going to do you?" I asked right before using the gun in my right hand to pistol whip her with the force of three men. As she fell violently against the wall and slid down the window pane, I straddled her body and aimed both of my weapons at her face for the kill shot.

"Remember when you asked me if you could shoot me?" I asked as my arms stiffened. As a trickle of blood slid down the side of her head, she managed to fix her eyes on mine through the daze I had sent her into.

"Did you really want to? No, did you *really* want to shoot me? Huh? Well what about now? Wanna borrow a gun? I just happen to have a couple handy."

Her heart was racing at a pace that would have allowed me to take her pulse just from watching her neck pound.

"For your sake, I hope you truly did. See you in hell…"

I simultaneously applied pressure to both triggers. There was a loud "bang", and all of the red instantly turned a blinding white...................

I opened my eyes… I looked around.........

"There is a tonic strength, in the hour of sorrow and affliction, in escaping from the world and society and getting back to the simple duties and interests we have slighted and forgotten. Our world grows smaller, but it grows dearer and greater. Simple things have a new charm for us, and we suddenly realize that we have been renouncing all that is greatest and best, in our pursuit of some phantom."

—*William George Jordan*

"Beware the fury of a patient man."— *John Dryden*